Winslow Hoffner's

HIGH-SAILING ADVENTURES

Book 2 *of the* Winslow Hoffner Series

MICHAEL THOMPSON

THOMPSON ORIGINAL PRODUCTIONS LLC

Published by Thompson Original Productions LLC
Bristow, Virginia, United States of America

Library of Congress Control Number: 2023916629

ISBN 978-1-954544-00-0 (Paperback)
978-1-954544-01-7 (eBook)

Written and Illustrated by Michael Thompson

Edited by William F. Kemp
Author Photo by Kara Thorpe
Beta Read by Daniela Eidelman,
Yaron Eidelman, and Forrest Rogers

For

Bill Kemp

*whose expertise in editing
brought my stories to new leagues.*

And for

Sam Yoder

*whose expertise in performance
brought my stories to new mediums.*

Contents

One o' the Classics 1

Dancin' with Fishfolk on Canvey Island 23

Monsters Are Real 37

Waking Up 61

Tales from the Trident 73

Troubled Waters 95

Trunko 119

The Way I Sees It 149

The Critter in the Crate 177

Hangar 19 and the Thingamajig 207

Out of the Dark 235

Always 257

The Everlovin' Loch Ness Monster 277

The Storyteller 301

About the Author 315

One o' the Classics

 a this day, I haven't the foggiest idea what this thing was…" the sailor reflected, rowing his small boat into the shimmering, blue expanse. Even with his head ducked low and his eyes squinted, he could still sense the warmth of his lady's presence. And when her lilted giggle rose over the splashing of paddles, he lifted his gaze to find her, lounging placidly on the bench before him.

A youthful breath empowered his chest, as the young Winslow Hoffner's eyes glittered on the most tender, humbling vision imaginable: the most remarkable woman he'd ever known.

He gallanted, "Maybe ya can wager a guess, Anna, yers is as good as mine."

Wavy, ruby tresses cascaded over her shoulders as she leaned in on the creaky, wooden bench and into the heavenly morning blush, haloed in sunrays. Her legs crossed under the flowing, sand-colored frills of her dress. On her higher knee, she rested an elbow; on her hand, she rested her chin; and on her lips, a gentle, pink smile dawned.

She replied, "I'd wager ye got yourself lost in that handsome head o' yours."

"Sorry." Winslow shook free. "I was... just realizin' how lucky I am."

"Oh, are ye *just* realizin' that?"

"Naw," Winslow assured her. "Just... realizin' it all over again, I s'pose." He grinned. "Maybe *that's* how the answer eluded me all this time. Ya kept distractin' me!"

Anna's daring, maritime eyes flashed with the magical reflections of daybreak on water. "Well, since ye find me so *fascinatin'*," she flipped her hair, "I guess it's up tae *me* tae dig up your answer, then." She sleuthed through a pack and surfaced with a book: wrinkled, tanned, uneven pages pressed haphazardly between weathered, leather flaps. "Exhibit A!" she declared, unlooping the ribbon that fastened it, as sunglow traced the title etched on its wooden plaque: *Journal of Curiosities.* "Maybe ye left yourself a clue somewhere, along the way…"

Randomly, she flipped to an entry, then giggled, amused by its heading. *"Dancin' with Fishfolk on Canvey Island,"* she narrated.

"Oh, yeah," Winslow snorted. He pushed back his cap, fingertips wandering through curls of messy, blond mane, as he found the adventure in his memory. "One o' the classics. I think it was—"

"Winter o' 1968!" Anna sprang, book in hand, doing a dramatic reading in her best Winslow Hoffner impression. Her sudden rise made the rowboat splash and teeter. Winslow flapped his arms for stability, but his wife balanced deftly amid the sway. She continued, "The sleet had settled fer a moment, n' a ghoulish, gray fog hung low on the estuary…"

Winslow swiped water from his blond beard and chuckled, "I don't sound nothin' like that!"

Anna went on, squinting her left eye and making her right one wider. "We was finally free o' that consarn research ship, y'see, n' at long last off ta the fun part: paddlin' ta shore at the heels o' a legend… *Arrgh!*"

Winslow hooted, "I ain't a pirate, Anna!" as his lady fell over on him, laughing.

"Aye, but you're a scallywag." She held his chin and pressed a warm kiss on his lips, then pushed off his chest, face squinched in his likeness. "Now quit kissin' yerself n' lemme read!"

Winslow sat back and laced his fingers. The phantom smells of salt and brine drifted through time, and the pull of those far-off waters felt nearer, as Anna read his own words back to him, translating the messy scrawls into a tale.

Fog parted in Winslow's mind, and Anna's fervent performance took him back, playing over his memories like the narration of an old movie:

We was at the heels o' a legend alright — a legend that ought not have heels! A walkin' fishfella by the moniker o' the Canvey Island Monster…

Winslow blinked, lost in thought, then jolted when a gloved hand suddenly wrapped over his shoulder.

The deep, baritone voice to whom it belonged spoke, "You realize we'd get there twice as fast if *you* paddled *too*."

Winslow rotated to his partner, another young man whose winded chest rose with the shield-shaped agency patch and its black, Saturn insignia. The seafarer touched a matching brand stitched onto his own uniform, then snapped free of his enchantment, laughing awkwardly.

"That how that works?" He dipped the oars. "Math weren't never my strong suit... 'Sides, ya were doin' such a good job, I didn't notice!"

"Oh yes, I'm sure I'll be an *Olympian* after this," the agent mumbled. Oars spiraled away the gray vapors to reveal the inky tides beneath, as their flimsy rowboat knocked and sloshed toward land in the wintry noir. *"You'd think the sailor would be a* dream *partner for this assignment..."*

"Name's Winslow, in case ya forgot."

"I remember. Giuseppe Scialpi."

"Aye, ya were there when I got the job! Put 'er there." The sailor offered an upside-down handshake over his shoulder, and the uneven paddles made the rowboat turn. "Here's ta our first field mission, eh!"

"Uh..." Scialpi stammered, then clapped the exchange with his left hand and shook, while his

right arm strained to resume order to the craft. He uttered a short wheeze and a harried laugh as the boat pivoted. "C'mon man, *row*."

"Alright, alright," Winslow chuckled. "Thought ya could use the practice is all. Ya been cooped up in that floatin' lab all this time…"

Scialpi's eyes lifted to the metal ship looming megalithically in the distance: the Charybdis. He swallowed hard, feeling surveilled. "You and me both."

The sailor's legs pressed and arms flexed vitally as he rowed. "Me, I been doin' this since knee-high." A chilled breeze swiped their backs as they cut through the waves. The lantern at the bow squeaked and tottered, the howling mist glittered by quicker in their small sphere of light, and the dark, daunting shape of the research vessel curtained in the heavy fog.

Scialpi's breaths cycled from those of relief to astonishment as they sped, struck by how much power the skinny man ahead of him could produce, when he wanted to. Scialpi attempted to simulate the technique, throwing his whole body into the motion. He felt like he was getting the hang of it.

"Ya look like a noodle, Scialpi."

"I'm going to kill you."

Only when the rowboat's prow grinded to a stop did they realize they'd struck land. They rose, waist high in the fog. Winslow took the lantern while Scialpi took a camera, and their silhouettes bobbed through the rippling vapors, tails of their black coats floating behind them.

As they trekked, they passed by an old treasure hunter, who was listening for beeps on his metal detector. Scialpi avoided eye contact, while Winslow gave an awkward nod. The man's lip curled at them as they trundled through his area and up the gray dunes to find a square perimeter marked off by caution tape, with an advanced, silver tent buffeting at its center. There, the agents traded enthusiasm, Scialpi rushing ahead while Winslow slowed and cocked his head at the odd setup.

Sure, I ain't claimin' ta be the most "covert" fella meself, but the suits might as well've put up a neon sign sayin', "Nothin' ta see here, folks!" So naturally everyone came runnin'. Ol' Holler was givin' 'em what'd become his classic schpeel too…

"We appreciate your interest in our specimen, but we'll have to ask you to respect the delicacy of our research and *move along...*" The calm cadence of Corwin Holler, a senior director of their British sister organization, rose over the rabbles of the beachside spectators.

Winslow's mouth shifted pensively as he listened, then turned to see the reflection of his ID wiggle across one of the examiner's goggles.

"American?" she asked, voice muffled by gear.

"Aye," Winslow nodded. When her brow arched behind the plastic, he tried again. "...Howdy?"

The caution tape lifted, rippling brightly against a colorless sky, as Winslow ducked beneath to join his partner in the tent.

The air inside was thick with fishy reek. Scialpi was gagging. He donned the first facemask offered; Winslow gave a small wave to decline the next. The sailor set down his lantern, brushed away a blond lock, and turned, following the cool, steady denials of the man outside, and the disputes of two insistent interruptors:

"We know wot we saw!" a young voice chimed.

"It had needles for teeth! N' suckers for feet!" another corroborated. "It's the Canvey Island Monster!" The crowd parted around a pair of boys on bicycles. The first, a pale, skinny one with messy black curls pressed under an oversized tweed hat went on, "My da tole me all 'bout it. One washed up 'ere years ago."

The second, a redheaded, huskier one in faded blue overalls, nodded in nervous concurrence. "There's fishfolk livin' on the island."

Winslow smiled, whispering, "*Smart kids.*"

Scialpi shushed him.

Holler knelt to ask their names.

"Liam," said the first.

"Huxley," said the second.

"And how old are you?"

"Eleven," said Liam.

"And a half!" added Huxley.

Holler chuckled, "A very imaginative age." He stood and strolled. "An *infectious* imagination."

The adults exchanged credulous looks and murmurs.

Noticing Winslow and Scialpi in the tent behind him, Holler gestured. "Monster or not, what you've found has garnered *international* interest! That's something to be proud of..."

Scialpi nodded affably, but Winslow's brow slanted and hands stayed buried in his pockets, as Liam and Huxley shrank into their bicycles. Relenting to the official account, the rest of the spectators dispersed into the chilly fog, leaving only the two boys sitting in shivering protest.

Holler knelt again. "So, why don't you pedal off now? No sense in catching a cold over a simple monkfish."

"No sense in putting a tent over one neither," chattered Liam.

Holler grimaced.

The silver passageway zipped vertically, its square, plastic window framing the young watchers outside.

"*There's always something,*" Holler sighed.

Scialpi shrugged. "Perhaps if they stay the course they'll become agents themselves one day."

Holler raised his hat to smooth his steely hair. "Perhaps."

Winslow muttered, "*Or the world stays black n' white fer 'em.*" He sniffed and lifted his chin to the operation. "So where's this 'monkfish?' "

"The one it was eating is on the table."

The Americans gawped, as a mangled, shredded fish corpse was uncovered by one of the examiners.

Holler added, "That's the *official* story anyway," before motioning for a black tarp to be drawn, unveiling the true body on the ground. Winslow's throat bobbed, while Scialpi fawned and fulled the bellows of his camera.

From a chilled, metal contraption, cold fog rose off a motionless, unknown animal: about two feet long from its head to its frog-like legs. Its eyes looked like empty glass spheres, its pale scales were crisscrossed with frost, and its mouth hung open in a gaping, gasping shape, lined with white, needly teeth, just like the boys had attested.

"A Canvey Island Monster," Holler presented. "Only the third specimen ever collected…" He went on to describe his team's discovery and joke how they initially thought the creature had two mouths, until they pried the half-eaten monkfish from its frozen jaws.   But to Winslow, his words faded, distant and distorted.

Somethin' weren't right. After all the dues I paid workin' in that consarn lab, lookin' at critters just like this'n, I kept hopin' this fieldwork woulda held somethin' different. Somethin' alive n' free, but this… this was more o' the same…

Winslow winced as he flipped to a clean sheet in his journal and started sketching, trying to draw life back into the creature. But a gloved hand set a photograph over the page to develop, Scialpi dubbing it "a good one for the file," as the ghostly image faded through. Winslow sighed.

Turns out we'd just traded one lab fer another…

Another pale camera flash spotted Winslow's vision. He rubbed his eyes, as the British crew swept up their research and their director spoke:

"I think CRYPTICA's *finest* can take it from here."

Honored, Scialpi straightened up and answered, "Yes, sir," then enthusiastically agreed that the specimen would be returned safely. As the tent's exit unzipped, Liam and Huxley leaned, desperate to glimpse the secrets therein.

Holler's eyes rolled. He added, "And make sure nothing other than the *official story* leaves the tent uncovered," pointing out the sleek, cylindrical canister that cradled the specimen.

"Of course," Scialpi said.

When Winslow didn't reply, Holler squinted. "Agent Hoffner?"

Winslow shook free. "Yeah?" He cleared his throat. "Yeah. Like he said. No problem." He saluted. "Holler at ya later, Holler."

Scialpi tensed.

Holler glowered, repeating, "*CRYPTICA's finest*," then left.

Scialpi pulled down his mask and scrambled for his partner. "You understand that was one of the directors of *PRIMAL*, don't you? The people we're supposed to *impress*?"

"Fer such a rock n' roll name they sure take things serious…"

"This *is* serious!" Scialpi clamored, showing his camera. "We have *proof* of a *legend*."

Winslow's ice-blue gaze floated from the frozen body to the boys beyond the square, plastic window. *"Ain't even our legend,"* he mumbled.

Thunder boomed, as Scialpi frowned to read his partner's features. "What's the matter?"

"Just…" Winslow scratched the back of his head. "I dunno. Somethin' don't feel right." He sighed. "Thought it'd be more fun is all."

"This *is* fun!" Scialpi's voice cracked. He cleared his throat and rubbed his neck.

Winslow guffawed, "Thanks pal, I needed that."

Scialpi pointed, about to retort, but paused when a sudden rush of heavy rain battered the crinkling canvas. His dark eyes traced the ruction. "Perhaps we should wrap up."

A misplaced, tropic warmth radiated outside. Feeling drawn to it, Winslow drifted to the door.

"Where are you going?"

"Cold in here."

"You aren't thinking of letting those *hoodlums* see anything—?"

"They ain't hoodlums."

"You didn't answer my question."

"I'm just gettin' some air, Scialpi—"

WHOOSH! When the door unzipped, a rogue current rushed in, flapping open the passageway and soaking the inside with hot rain. Photos and papers were flung in the wild spiral while droplets pattered the uncovered body, spraying away the grit in its gills and the frost on its face.

Scialpi spluttered and wrestled with the flap. Winslow could hear him raging, but the winds puffing through the warping walls harmonized like heralding horns, and the tiny gasps of Liam and Huxley drowned out everything.

The sailor dragged his drenched hair from his eyes to behold their faces, alit with wonder. He smiled, but balked at a new noise behind him: a groggy, clicking croak. Rigid, he and Scialpi rotated to behold the tent's third resident.

It rose on shaky legs. A flux of warm, rosy health returned to the scales on its back. There, small, webby, red fins articulated; accordion-like gills of the same color flexed on its neck; a steamy breath chattered from an underbitten jaw; and thawed, cobalt eyes were moistened by the laps of a long, sticky tongue.

Reanimated, the Canvey Island Monster staggered upright on webbed, suction cup-like feet and made a clicky croak at the sight of its half-eaten meal on the table.

Scialpi shuddered, "It's... *alive?*" then fidgeted as the creature took a stiff hop, balancing on the edge of the metal canister meant to contain it. It launched a lengthy, frog-like tongue to grapple the dead monkfish and reel the carcass in, belly ballooning to engorge it, then glowing warmly like a small furnace.

"There goes the official story," Winslow commented.

Scialpi paled in panic.

"I knew it was real!" a small voice exulted. Liam and Huxley were suddenly right behind them.

"Get *out* of here!" Scialpi roared. He dove for the canister, but the Canvey Island Monster let out a spooked squeal and sprang, webbed feet slapping off Scialpi's face as it bounded to seize freedom outside. Liam and Huxley cheered and pedaled after the pink blur.

"N' there goes the *unofficial* story!"

Scialpi growled, flailing sand as he snagged the metal canister and they took to the chase. The headlights of the children's chiming bikes beamed on their fleeing subject.

Scialpi wheezed, "*This – is – a nightmare!*"

"This's more like it!" Winslow hurrahed at his side.

"Are you *insane?!*"

The sprinting men, pedaling kids, and whooping, bounding beast silhouetted against a thawing sky. They seemed to have outrun the sudden rainfall, but the fog ahead of them steamed, rising to eye-level.

View obscuring and bicycle tracks being lapped by waves, Scialpi panted, "It's getting away!"

Through a swirl in the mist they briefly reunited with the old treasure hunter, who was cursing and climbing from a fruitless dig.

"*Rubbish!*" he grumbled, chucking his shovel and malfunctioning metal detector beside an empty hole and stomping off.

Scialpi's eyes flashed, trading the canister with his partner and searching his pockets. He took out a clunky, rectangular instrument.

"What's that?" Winslow asked.

Scialpi periscoped two antennae and turned a dial, as the gadget hummed to life. "A prototype."

Under a glass dome, a compass-like needle swiveled. It clicked to face them. Scialpi frowned, looking over his shoulder, then hammered the side of the machine. It pointed forward and beeped.

"There!"

They puffed past the haywire metal detector and fussing, foaming waves at the direction of the mysterious tool, finding themselves beneath the creaky beams of a dark pier. There, they rediscovered the boys' bike lights cutting through the dense vapors.

"There they—"

The bikes blew past them.

"—*go?*"

"Leg it!" Huxley wailed to his friend.

"Good luck," Liam panted to the agents.

The gusts from the escapees rattled their coats, as the prototype machine whirred, overheating.

Ahead, two white spots ignited, brighter than those of the fleeing bikes: the glowing eyes of the monster. Winslow tried to radio HQ, but only a clatter of static came back. In tandem, the needle of

Scialpi's strange gadget whizzed, pointing everywhere. Their heads darted to chase the readings, but found nothing but creaking wood and gushing waves. A glowing mouth opened next with a call that matched the sound of the pier's old, swaying posts. Winslow and Scialpi backed, then blanched, when the waves stilled, but the creaking continued, vibrating everywhere, swelling, alive.

The eyes of the Canvey Island Monster glowed brighter, casting haunting beams through the shadowed fog.

Then, countless others opened.

Dancin' with Fishfolk
on Canvey Island

 *ow, even t'day Scialpi'll claim this never happened. But what yer readin' now, this right here... this's the absolute truth...*

The device exploded. Giuseppe Scialpi grunted and chucked it. From the fog, a tongue lashed out, sticking to the discarded item, and reeled. A new creature, this one larger with a glowing lure on its head akin to that of an anglerfish, gobbled the hot metal and flumped into sight, mouth fuming.

As more slinked from above and skulked from the sides, the radio in the young Winslow Hoffner's hand crackled with a collage of voices from various frequencies, even intercepting the voice of a talk show host announcing, *"We're back, folks!"* before another tongue launched from the fog to nab it.

"They're hungry," Winslow gulped.

More emerged, peeling from the timber of the pier, slogging from the waves of the estuary. Some even shuffled up from the sand below their feet. They were surrounded.

From above, a little one dropped onto Scialpi's shoulder, cheeping, eyes and mouth both lit up. It licked him, and he shivered and swatted it.

"Get off!"

The youngling made a small *peep* as it bounced to the rest of its clan. They growled.

"Oh, no."

Winslow pulled Scialpi's arm. "Run."

Against an amethyst sky, the shapes of the two men bounded to escape the tumbling mass of gurgling, toothy beasts.

The tribe of monsters caught up, swelling like a wave around the stupefied pair. The metal canister dropped from Winslow's grip, and enough of the croaking clan managed to swarm their might against Scialpi to sweep him off his feet. He yelped, coasting over their heads like a crowd surfer.

"Nonono!" He kicked. His attempts to escape were thwarted by the group effort of the tiny beasts, who swiftly sluffed him into the dusty ditch left by the treasure hunter. Scialpi spat out grit, then shot up, chest-deep in the hole. "Winslow!" he called. "Help—*uff!*"

Sand was slapped backward by multiple webbed feet, and in a blink, Scialpi was buried up to his neck.

"I'm comin'!" Winslow called, working his way through the horde. "Just, ah… hang tight?"

"I don't have any choice!"

The chattering creatures patted the sand down, securing him.

Winslow hopped and sidled. "Almost there—!"

Several tongues flung, slathering Scialpi's bald head with a thick coat of glistening slime.

"Dear, God! Winslow, they're going to eat me!"

"Hang on, pal!" Winslow pressed. Ahead, one nuzzled in driftwood, and another hacked up a glittery deposit over the tinder. *"What're they—?"*

Eyes, mouths, and lures lit up. Scialpi squinted under the shine and sweated under the heat. The vocalizations of the little horrors blended, and the metal detector by Scialpi's ear whirred and rang, as Winslow staggered for his partner and shielded his eyes, reaching. Scialpi screamed, ducking, and at that angle, his sheened crown fused the creature's lights into a single, focused beam.

FWOOSH! Driftwood ignited. Scialpi panted. The tribe of fishfolk bounced in glee around their new campfire, less vicious, and Winslow fell on his back in laughter.

Scialpi roared, "Tell *no one* of this!"

Winslow hooted and held his ribs, his laughs syncing with those of his future self.

He rolled over in the rowboat, wiping tears, as Anna joined him.

"Winslow, there's *no way* this happened!"

"I'm tellin' ya!" he squealed.

"But *how* – ?"

"I dunno!"

Anna's brow scrunched in disbelief and hilarity, finger pointing to the impossible account on the page before breaking into a fit of giggles herself. "How come ye never told me?"

"I was sworn ta silence," Winslow squeaked.

"And ye kept that pledge all this time?"

"Oh, I'd say it's still goin'." Winslow coughed. "Ya may've read it, but technically I didn't tell."

She tackled him with a hug and they laughed together, the Journal of Curiosities fanning to a page that featured an illustration of a dancing Canvey Island Monster. Below it were less decipherable notes and a cryptic series of arrow-shaped glyphs.

"What're these?"

"Oh," Winslow chuckled and wiped his eye. "That's the dance."

"The dance?"

"Aye."

Anna flipped for further details but couldn't find any. "What's the dance?"

Winslow shook his head with a smile.

"Tell me!"

"Well, turned out these fishfolk were quite the party animals. Scialpi musta thought I was goofin'. Guess fer a moment I was—I got distracted by this li'l purple guy. Looked kinda familiar somehow...

"I said, 'Ey, Scialpi! I think I know this'n!'

"N' he groaned, 'Fascinating.'

"But I was serious. It looked different than the others—had some extra fins here n' there, n' was a li'l less hyper. I said, 'Look at him! Looks like he dances when he walks.'

"N' Scialpi shouted, 'Dance over here and *help me!*'" Winslow shook his head. "Poor fella. He didn't know how right he was. 'Cause soon as he said that, the whole beach broke inta a bash! The beasties started singin'... in a way." Winslow snorted. "Let's just say they was better dancers than singers. Afore I knew it, I was bumped inta the groove o' this li'l critter conga line, circlin' the fire. Scialpi weren't too pleased. But ta be fair, there wasn't much I could do! They was everywhere. N' if ya weren't in rhythm, ya weren't with 'em. So, I went at it."

He stood to demonstrate, the rocky, clunking floor wobbling oddly as he stomped, shimmied, shuffled, and skipped. Anna squinched, lake water sprinkling on her nose.

Winslow brought his elbows up. "They didn't have no arms so I added this part." He waggled a finger and turned.

Anna clapped, and her sailor bowed and joined her on the bench. Finding an edge, she peeled one page free from another to reveal the conclusion.

"Oh! Here's the rest of it!" she rejoiced, clearing her throat:

Turns out there was more ta this ritual than just a bit o' fun. When the fire went out, some o' the bigger fishfolk laid eggs in the warm ash. Guess this whole thing was a baby shower…

On the beach, Winslow sat and sketched—finding the same creature from the tent had lingered for a while afterward, particularly lively. The young sailor breathed in the salt and petrichor on the dewy breezes, then waved to the little legends as they tossed sand and ash over their eggs and scuttled into the foam of the estuary, lit with gold and ruby tones from the setting sun. He clapped his journal shut.

Scialpi watched with beleaguered scorn as every specimen vanished, too tired to protest. His partner strolled over.

"Quite the party," he said, eyes still fixed on the dusking waves of the Thames, lost in whimsy.

Scialpi's slime- and sand-coated head rotated to view him, as a wave raked near. He shivered. "Just get me out of here."

"Sure thing." Winslow started digging.

"*All that*," Scialpi fumed, "*and not a shred of evidence.*"

"What're ya talkin' 'bout?" Winslow showed his journal. "Got the whole thing right here! First-hand account. Clan behavior, vocalizations. N' how 'bout that nestin' ritual!"

"Believe me, I had an unfortunate view."

"Yer gonna laugh about this one day," Winslow promised him. He chuckled. "Remember when ya thought they was gonna eat ya?"

Scialpi's frown deepened.

Winslow gulped. "Ya peeved?"

"No."

"Ya seem peeved."

"I'm fine."

Winslow studied him. "If I were ta leave ya in there a li'l longer —"

"*Winslow...*"

" — would ya be twice as calm or twice as mad?"

Scialpi growled, and when a small wave swiped in and loosened the sand, he punched an arm free.

" 'Course math weren't never my strong suit."

Scialpi shambled from the ground and chased.

Winslow bounded for the rowboat, impish laughs trailing, "*Hoo hoo hoo!*"

The agent abandoned the pursuit, seeing the sailor reach the boat in record time and hearing him tease from afar, "*I'll come back fer ya when ya don't want me dead!*"

Scialpi's chest fell with a pant. He doubled back to collect the empty specimen canister. He groaned, but an ember's pop drew his dark eyes to the ash pile, and an idea.

Dusting away a layer, he reached in, then delicately transferred something to his case.

"*That'll do…*" he mumbled.

The specimen canister clunked as he twisted the handles, locking its contents with a freezing hiss, as ice frosted over a soft, webby egg.

Scialpi rose, holding the case at his waist and adjusting his grimy, yellow tie as he glimpsed his partner hooting on the rowboat just offshore.

In it, Winslow dropped into a lay, rocking in the base of the boat, laughing.

In a future time, Anna lay beside him, head resting on his chest as she leafed through the journal's pages.

She cuddled up to him snugly. "Promise me we'll spend every anniversary on a lake as braw n' bonnie as this'n."

"Ya got it," the sailor avowed. "I'll mark every calendar."

Anna's cheeks dimpled as she admired the illustrations in her husband's journal. "Any clues?"

"Hm? 'Bout what?" Winslow turned to glimpse her in the dawning rays.

"That mystery ye were lookin' tae solve," Anna reminded him.

"Oh," Winslow's eyes fluttered. "That's right."

Anna sighed.

The sailor admitted, "I was so wrapped up in the thing I guess I forgot..." With one hand he stroked her back. With the other he touched the doodles in his margins: of the Canvey Island Monsters' glow, and of the malfunctioning prototype Scialpi brought, retroactively labeled, *Cryptolabe*.

"Any inklin'?" Anna asked.

"*Yeah…*" Winslow murmured. His cheek rubbed her rosy hair as the shimmering lake swayed them. His chest rising, he felt them breathe as one. "But, I gots a feelin' this mystery goes back even further…"

"Well, I'm all ears. Here…" Anna passed him his journal. "Your turn." She snuggled up. "No offense, but your voice is tough on the throat."

Winslow laughed serenely, flipped the page, and drifted through memories. Finding the perfect starting point, he perked up, excited, and asked, "Up fer another one?"

His lady's eyes met his with an adoring sparkle. She answered, "Always."

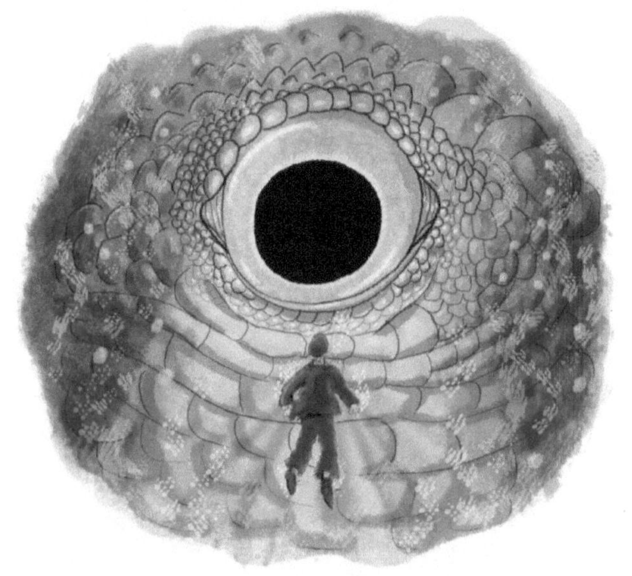

Monsters Are Real

ut with it, Wins!"

"*What?*" The old fisherman blinked. He caught himself staring deeply into the vibrant watercolor of a dreamy lake and a cozy rowboat, framed on the dark, walnut wall of Keeley's Bayside Eatery.

The restaurant's namesake went on, "Ye keep enticin' us then driftin' off again!"

"*Driftin' – !*"

"Not now, Sleepy. He ain't even started yet!"

Winslow Hoffner sat back on his creaking barstool, rediscovered his audience, then cracked a sly grin. "Did I just hear ya call me stories *enticin'*?"

Ken Keeley's face flushed. "*Ooh,* I oughtta—"

The silver bun of his small mother, Muirin, skated around the corner of the bar. Her blue eyes peeked up to flash daggers at him over the counter.

Ken glanced left to see two blond youngsters, Lily and her brother Luke, kicking their feet merrily over the edge of their seats beside their mother, Linda Cunningham, as they awaited the seafarer's newest story.

Ken sighed, tipped his head, and conceded, gesturing with cheeky grandiosity as he rephrased, "*...Ask...* ye kindly to entertain us."

The kids bounced with an overflow of enthusiasm. So did the eatery's regulars.

Sal "Sleepy" Hurly reached across the counter to shake Ken's arm. "That's the spirit, Ken! *That's* the spirit!"

Muirin's expression softened and eyes twinkled with approval as she returned, presented the kids with fishsticks, then coasted through the packed space to deliver more orders.

"Alrighty," Winslow clapped. "Fuel me up!"

Dark, sugary bubbles gushed to replenish his glass of root beer, and the fisherman took a big swig, licked the corner of his mouth, then leapt from his seat in a spry gallop.

"It was a night like any other I reckon. Cool, crisp. Waters weren't too rough neither; we was pullin' in a hefty catch. Still, somethin' weren't right." His buggy eye quivered at his excited listeners. Townsfolk from all of Bayfield had clustered to hear the latest account from the local legend, and he was happy to oblige.

"Maybe it was the stars..." He moved his fingers mystically at the high, wood ceiling, which Ken had appropriately decorated with strings of small, amber bulbs. "They was oddly colorful that night. Looked like them constellations were puttin' on a light show. Saw a couple o' *shootin'* stars too!" He paced by the window, outside of which the bay's foaming waves lapped. "Or, maybe we was just on edge. Weren't but a couple moons back when the *Kraken* came ta visit our bay, keep in mind..."

Ken crossed his thick arms and chewed a toothpick. "Pretty healthy turnaround time for a sequel, eh?"

Winslow winked. "Aye, fate has an odd way o' showin' herself." He sipped and smiled, buzzing with an honored warmth at the intent focus of his livened listeners. "Whatever it was—some force o' nature, some..." he shook his head, "*energy* was

41

pressin' down on Hank n' me, n' we just knew it. Somethin' impossible was about ta happen."

Questions rose over the excited murmurs:

"What do ye *mean?*"

"What *energy?*"

"What did it *feel* like, Wins?"

Winslow sipped and smacked, staring off, then answered, "Felt like a young'un again. Grippin' me sheets close at night, watchin' the closet, Momma tellin' me there weren't nothin' ta worry about, 'cause monsters ain't real…"

"Momma Hoffner sounds like a smart woman," Ken ragged.

Winslow noticed the wide eyes of the children and the heads of the adults tilting in anticipation. He cleared his throat.

"She was." He nodded. " 'N she was right!"

Ken frowned. "Really?"

"Aye. There weren't nothin' ta worry about." Winslow finished his root beer, heavy glass mug clunking as he set it down and wiped his beard on his sleeve. His right eye glittered at the crowd. "But monsters *are* real."

From perfectly still, black waters mirroring an incandescent night sky, an otherworldly beast beset the Seanna. The reflected stars rippled apart like a million liquid supernovas, boiled by foam. It emerged — what looked like the tail of a gargantuan cosmic whale with three flukes — and the captain and his first mate were catapulted and carried off by the resultant wave.

The harrowing account manifested in ink, wreathing a blurry, but bold photograph of a trident-shaped tail breaking the waves, and was garlanded by an even bolder title:

"*Monsters Are Real*," the headline was read aloud in the Australian cadence of the assistant editor. When his coaly eyes steadied on the names of the shared byline, his nostrils flared, and he flopped the proof copy onto his boss' desk. "Bit of a brazen statement, don'tcha think, Al?"

Albert Nguyen set his elbows on the antique mahogany and tapped his fingers in thought. "Perhaps," he relented. "But it is eye-catching. I like it."

"Is that all that matters now? You know online they have a word for titles like that. *Clickbait*," Nell Dunney fumed, pacing. " 'Course you can't even commit to digital enough to even let us have *that* honor."

Becci Hamrin shot from her chair in defense. "It's a *pullquote*, Nell, not a declaration from the paper. And the full quote appears in the lede. There's nothing misleading about it."

"Are you *kidding* me —?"

"I understand both sides," Albert raised his hands to calm them. "It's a matter of perspective." He glanced at Nell. "Of preference."

"And *you* prefer *this*." Nell prodded the paper. "Fantasy."

"Now, hang on there —"

"No *you* hang on, Al," Nell shook, pointing. "You're my friend and I respect you, but this has gone too far. I'm trying to save us from further embarrassment."

"*Embarrassment?*" Becci scoffed.

Nell ignored her.

She stepped closer. "Do *awards* embarrass you?"

He groaned.

"Or is it just the ones *you* don't win?"

Nell grinned darkly. *"Easy, Beck..."*

"Becci, that's enough," Albert reprimanded. "We may have differences of opinion, but we're a family." The editor-in-chief's forehead wrinkled in concern. "This paper belongs to all of us."

"Couldn't agree more," Nell lauded, strolling to the side of the wide, stately desk and leaning. "All I'm saying is we need to get back to basics. To the *news.*"

There was a beat of silence. Becci contained her ire and breathed. Albert sighed. Nell forged a smile under his sour eyes, then drew a lollipop from a jar on the editor-in-chief's desk. It was purple. His lip curled at it, and he sifted for another.

"What do you think, John?" Albert asked.

Heads rotated to the yet-unspoken fourth participant in the meeting, sitting in a green, vinyl chair against the far wall. Becci's olivine eyes honed in on him, trying to read his mind.

Nell squinted, crinkling the packaging of the purple lollipop and muttering, "Yeah, what say you, Johnny?" He ripped the plastic begrudgingly. "You've been oddly quiet."

John Chaplain took a long breath through his nose, thinking, then spoke, "I like what we wrote. I wouldn't change it." He swallowed dryly. "But, I understand Nell's concerns over the headline. We can make it something a little more..." He searched for the right word. "Ambiguous?"

Becci smiled. "I'm cool with that. A rose by any other name, right?"

John nodded. "Right. Winslow likes more of a mysterious tone anyway. I think Nell's instincts are right. It'll be truer to his account."

Nell squinted and grinned slyly.

"Seems like a fair compromise," Albert wagered. "Would you agree, Nell?"

The heads of the room swiveled his way.

"It's the content I'm concerned about." When Becci straightened up to interject he lifted his hand. "Nothing on the writing, just the subject matter. Call me a skeptic, but—"

Albert interjected, "If I may." His eyes twinkled as he held up the page and pointed to the photo of the unknown monster's trident-shaped tail. "This photograph came courtesy of an independent archivist."

"Milly Matterhorn," Nell said.

"Yes! And it was published *decades* ago in the New Highlands Herald."

"And?"

"Doesn't this mean there's something there? That there's precedent?"

"There's something there," Nell nodded. "I'm just not sure it's news." His nostrils flared. "I'm not sure it's *real*."

"The photograph?"

"Any of it! The fire-breathing fish, the giant octopus—"

Becci argued, "We were *there*, Nell!"

"I don't blame you for getting caught up in the whimsy, Beck. It's a charming delusion. But think. Really. Think! This bloke has a once in a lifetime experience, what… once a *month*? How's that even possible? Who's to say he isn't making this whole thing up?!"

"I say yer makin' this whole thing up!" Keeley challenged.

Winslow shrugged. "Ya can say that, but it don't change what happened."

"What did happen, Mr. Hoffner?" Luke asked.

"I'll tell ya!" Winslow said. "Seemed like the whole ocean turned upside-down on us." A fresh root beer fizzed under his chin. "After the wave came, I couldn't see nothin' but black... felt like I was floatin' in outer space. Chunks o' rock n' sediment was twirlin' by me like *comets* no less. I was in trouble. So, I started swimmin' fer the surface with all the strength I had. Problem was, I didn't know which way was up!"

Winslow mimed his aching progression. "No air, no light, n' no sense o' direction. I pulled n' kicked hard as I could, but this crushin' cold came over me, n' I felt the bubbles from me mouth twirl downward the other way."

Winslow's sight cast over his rigid listeners. "Turns out down was up," he revealed. "I'd been workin' me way deeper this whole time..."

The children made tiny gasps.

Sleepy clambered over the counter, drink sloshing. "We almost lost us a legend!"

"Oh, *brother.*" Ken rolled his eyes.

"I dunno 'bout all *that*, Sleepy. But I do know I was certainly 'bout ta find one." Winslow shot up. "The darkness seemed ta peel." His buggy, right eye quivered at the crowd. "It was the beastie's eye! A huge, dark circle set in a glowin' orange ring. If the abyss was outer space, her eye was an undersea solar eclipse. It was the size o' this room! Ain't *never* seen an eye that big!"

"Have ye seen a mirror?" Ken teased. "*Ach!*" A sharp jab in his ribs shushed him, and his head darted to see his mother a considerable distance away. He paled. "*How did ye…?*"

She blew her finger like a smoking revolver. "Be nice to yer friend, Kenny!"

Winslow smirked. "Momma Keeley's a smart woman."

Ken crossed his arms again, red face cycling emotions.

"Turns out this beastie was a momma too!" Winslow picked up. "I could hear a whole pod of 'em hummin' a tune, caught glimpse of a young'un's tail chasin' guppies in the light o' the momma's eye." A hard wind rushed against the howling boards, rattling the soft orange bulbs above and highlighting the storyteller's intensity. "I was so in awe, I forgot I had ta breathe!"

The room gasped and laughed.

"I forgot again when I saw Hank hoverin' close by. Started swimmin' fer 'im. Didn't have time ta close the distance though, 'cause the momma dove under both of us, n' puffed. The whole ocean turned white!

"Two blowholes the size o' volcanoes went spoutin'. There was more air than water then. Somehow I caught me breath. Hank did too. Could hear him gurglin' somethin' at me, but I couldn't tell what."

The front door clunked open and as if on cue, the first mate entered the restaurant. He shook off the chill and pulled off his jacket. "Ahoy, folks!"

Everyone clapped.

He smiled. "What a welcome!"

"Wins is tellin' us 'bout yer latest bout with fate!" Sleepy explained. "The tale o' the... eh, what was it again?"

"Don't say nothin' more!" Ken butted in. "We've a rare opportunity to fact-check the man!"

"Would ya bet a drink on it?" Sleepy burbled.

"Yeah, fine. Whatever."

"Hank! Ken's got a question!"

"Fire away, Kenster."

The cook pointed, "What *creature* did ye n' Wins see the other day?"

Hank squinted. "The biggest."

"The descriptions match!" Sleepy raised a glass.

"That ain't—!" Ken's face turned bright crimson. "The species, Hank! What *kind?!*"

"Oh."

All leaned in, chairs creaking.

Hank thought hard. He answered, "Dunno."

"In all fairness she was a hard critter ta place," Winslow said.

"An' too big tae see all o' her!"

"Aye. Ya could look left n' right n' never get a full picture!"

"No hints!" Ken squeaked.

"*Hm.*" Hank pondered. "Hard tae say, Ken. We's hopin' tae find her again one day n' get a better look. From what I saw, she wore a bit o' everythin'. Scales here, fur there."

Winslow was about to agree again, but Ken shushed him and leaned in. "*What. Did. Ye. See?*"

Hank's cheeks puffed in thought. He shook his head. "Can't say for sure what she was, Ken. Though, tae me, it felt like the most familiar thing, like I'd seen her somewhere before in pages, or heard whispers o' her in some olden tale, somewhere. Maybe..." His eyes floated to the ceiling, where the orange bulbs swayed dreamily. "Maybe it's just an instinct we sailors have. There's no finer testament tae the size o' this Earth than bein' at sea, with no land on either side o' ye. A whole different world. An' for that dominion, I'd say there's no finer queen. I can only hope one day we catch a better look, tae pay our respects proper!" His face glittered with a magical candor. "This beastie, whatever she was, she has in her a soul as ancient n' mysterious as all the Earth's waters."

The room was enchanted, but Ken was firm in his skepticism. "So no specifics."

"No' really." Ken was about to claim victory, until Hank added, "No' till her glowin' eye opened, that is."

Excited whispers filled the room.

Ken blanched.

"Her pupil was the size o' the bar! An' a ring o' orange glowed 'round it… like a…" He snapped his fingers. "Like a…"

"*Eclipse?*" Ken mumbled.

"Aye, tha's it!"

The room erupted in ebullient applause.

Ken looked dumbstruck, but was shaken alert when Sleepy waggled his empty tankard. He refilled it, swearing the fishermen must've coordinated the detail, as Winslow chuckled and patted his first mate's back.

Hank gestured to the lively uproar around them. "Sounded a bit like this when the momma's blowholes jetted under us. Lucky she had one for each of us, eh?"

"Aye, I'd say so," Winslow rejoined. "What was ya shoutin' at me, by the way?"

"Oh, I was just shoutin' for shoutin's sake."

"Ah, fair 'nough."

"*Alright,*" Ken relented. "Go on."

The engrossed crowd formed a tighter ring as Winslow described how they emerged from the abyss at shocking speeds to behold the Seanna skating on a high wave.

"The timin' was perfect," Winslow said, illustrating the boat's descent with one hand and their rise with the other. "By the momma's tail, the boat came coastin' down."

"*Coastin'!*" Sleepy gushed, drinking.

"Up front, me n' Hank was ridin' the momma's spouts like a livin' geyser."

"You *geyser* lucky! *Ha!*" Sleepy drank.

"When the boat lined up with us... I practically just walked on."

"I ended up in the nets," Hank admitted.

The crowd chuckled.

"N' then, the momma's tusks broke the froth."

"Oh, yeah!"

"Tusks?" Ken frowned.

"Aye," Winslow attested.

"Nearly took ma trousers!" Hank guffawed.

"Sharp towers o' ivory," Winslow described.

"She n' her babes gobbled the whole catch! Sawed through the nets in one pass!"

"Never *saw* such a thing," Winslow joked. He looked to Sleepy, but he was snoring. "Oh." Winslow shrugged. "Tough day fer fishin' t'be sure, but I s'pose the momma was just lookin' out fer her babes, like all good mommas do."

"That's right," Linda Cunnigham chimed.

"That's right," Muirin echoed, collecting dishes and patting her son's back as she passed.

"I managed ta get Hank free just as the beasties' trident-tails flapped off. One last wave roared under the boat n' carried us back ta the marina in a blink. N' we wobbled there all drenched, lookin' o'er the still waters that rippled like nothin' ever happened."

"Even the bay don't believe ye," Ken teased.

"Oh, I dunno 'bout that, Keel."

"Aye," Hank said. "Take a look a' the waves next chance ye get. I'd say they're sittin' a tad lower."

Listeners squeezing against the window agreed:

"I thought something was off!"

"You see that rock? That's a new rock for sure!"

Lily and her brother's eyes widened. "That's how big they were!" she gasped.

Winslow toasted. "The biggest."

The crowd hurrahed and pumped glasses. The kids mimicked the action with their juice cups. Winslow polished off his root beer with a satisfied breath.

Ken couldn't help but smile. "Ye sure can weave a tale," he admitted.

Winslow shrugged. "It's what we do."

"Aye," Hank nodded. "We's in the business o' guts an' gallantry."

Ken shifted his toothpick to the corner of his mouth. "Speakin' o' business," he thought aloud, "is this tale an elaborate excuse for last week's late delivery?"

Hank and Winslow traded glances, then said:

"This don' change our paycheck does it?"

"Aye, if anythin' that whale's yer best customer."

The fishermen chuckled and scurried off as Ken slapped the counter.

Sleepy's head shot up at the noise. He smacked his parched gums and took a look around the bare room, then glimpsed his empty tankard. " 'Ey Ken, where's m'refill?"

"Ye downed it already."

Sleepy wobbled. "I don' remember that."

"The bet was honored, buddy, I promise..." Ken gestured for corroboration, but the restaurant was blank. His arms slapped back to his sides.

"Mm." Sleepy sniffed. "Bit hard to believe."

"Oh, is *that* too far-fetched for ye?"

The tankard filled again as the regular thanked him and dozed beside it. Ken wiped down the bar, watching his customers' happy shapes reveling outside as they made their way home.

"Maybe there's somethin' to it," he said.

"Heard that!" Muirin called.

"I ain't sayin' I believe it!" he defended.

Sleepy snorted in slumber, hand tossing in the direction of a framed cutout of the Giganteus story.

"This town's fulla dreamers."

Heads pounding and voices rasping, the journalists adjourned their meeting.

"Enter the changes tonight," Albert passed the draft to John. "We go to print tomorrow."

John's throat knotted. Entire sections were crossed out. A hit list of edits was bulleted in the margins, all penned by Nell.

"I'll take care of it."

"Shoot me an email when it's fixed," Nell said.

Fixed, John and Becci shared a thought. They held their tongues, as the assistant editor held the door for them. Becci left first.

In parting, John offered, "Sorry about how heated things got. We just want the story to be perfect."

Albert nodded in approval.

Nell tilted his head. He unwrapped a second grape lollipop and bit it, smiling with purple teeth. "Apology accepted." He backed inside, and the office door thumped shut.

John lingered, then swallowed hard and joined Becci in a haunting, echoey walk down the dark halls.

"Did you just apologize to *him?*"

John sighed, "Trying to keep the peace."

Becci squinted down the hall at the red exit sign looming dimly above the doors. "I don't think we want *Nell's* idea of peace."

John considered the sentiment and watched the wriggling, pale lights gliding over the floor, as his loafers clapped across its slick tiles. "I know," he said, "but he *is* the assistant editor." He reviewed the pages of their story again. The trident-shaped tail of the awe-inspiring, unknown whale tossed in the bay, while a massacre of red edits bled all around it.

Becci shook her head. "We're swimming with sharks, J-Chap."

Waking Up

lumes of foam spiraled through the black. The surface steamed, rippling in ring-shaped portals with every heavy thud, until a bigger disturbance rattled the surface into spitting, searing froth.

"*Ah!*" the journalist recoiled as a sprinkle of hot coffee skipped from his cup onto his arm.

Midway through the transfer of her notepad, laptop, and stacks of bulky research from her arms to the café table, Becci Hamrin froze. "*Sorry,*" she grimaced, setting the rest down in slow-motion.

John licked his wrist, "All good," as a barista hurried to their aid.

"Sorry, that's the wiggly table," the woman groaned, promptly swiping away the mess, then bunching napkins under the uneven table leg.

"There." She brushed a distressed, snow-blond lock behind her ear. "Can I get you a new cup?"

"Oh, no no, it's alright. It didn't spill too much."

"You sure?" Dark eyebrows crested over her crystal blue eyes.

"Uh, yeah," John said. "I'm good. Thanks."

"Okay," she smiled back.

Becci studied the exchange behind her reading specs and glimpsed the nametag of the lingering barista. "Thanks, Winter, we're all set."

"Okay," she repeated, same smile plastered. "Just, uh..." She swung her foot and backstepped. "Let me know if you change your mind!" Her sky-colored skirt swished as she spun back behind the counter.

John went for a sip. "Friendly place."

"She likes you," Becci said.

John coughed. "What?"

Squares of green light glowed on the lenses before Becci's sly eyes, as her computer booted up. "She thinks you're cute." She sipped and typed something. "She'll probably give you her number, if you don't mess it up first."

"You really think... Wait, *mess it up*?"

"You know. Get all weird."

"I'm weird?"

Becci started laughing through her nose.

She's messing with me. John smiled and shook his head, flipping open his notepad, then pressed, "I'm *weird?*"

"Only when you go into full-mailroom vampire mode." She clicked open a document. "Trapped in your own head. Flustered, twitchy."

"I don't—" He nearly jumped from his chair when Winter popped back in with a menu.

"*Ooh,* sorry to scare you!"

"I-I wasn't—"

"Here you go. Sorry."

"No prob—uh, thank you." John sighed, as the barista disappeared again and Becci giggled:

"Maybe I shouldn't have said anything."

That was needlessly awkward, John thought. He took a breath to steady himself, embarrassment melting in the roasty, soothing aroma of the small coffee bar. Its name, *Brite n' Earlie's,* glowed in warm neon outside, beneath a 30's-style cartoon of two figures: an anthropomorphized, caffeinated sun, winking one of its pie-shaped eyes with a cheesy grin, and hoisting a steamy mug in one gloved hand while giving a big thumbs-up with the other, beside a drowsy cloud-character with a cumulous mustache, who looked to be just waking up. The glass door chimed as patrons moseyed in. They loosed their scarves in comfy reprieve and settled into the red-and-white booths of the semi-retro café.

"Business," John changed the subject.

"Yes," Becci said. "Did you bring it?"

"Yes." John reached into his pocket, fingers touching the cool, metal chain. He swallowed and checked over his shoulder.

"No one's gonna know what it is," Becci assured him.

John nodded, and the chain rattled as he drew the instrument. An octagonal, brassy, navigational device twirled on the other end, beveled with the Saturn insignia of the monster hunters they encountered on the bay. The Cryptolabe.

When the symbol on the center of the top lid was pressed, the gadget unlocked and sprang open like a clamshell on squeaking, old hinges, displaying a purple, compass-like needle under a glass dome, bordered by bulbs of a matching color. And inside the lid, the inscription, *Property of* CRYPTICA, was etched.

"Thanks for getting a jump on the research for this story, Becci."

"Thanks for staying up late to '*fix*' our last story."

"*Mm*-hm." John's chest tightened at the word, Nell's dig still fresh in their minds.

In sync, Becci smiled sardonically and shivered away the past. "Happy thoughts." She typed a little harder. "We're on to the next one now."

"Agreed." John sipped his coffee, buzzing back to the present. "Did you find anything on the group?"

"Uh-huh." Becci pulled up a page. "Well... sort of. It's odd." She turned the screen and showed a picture of an educational center with the same logo prominently displayed on its signage.

"What...?"

"*Yeah*," Becci said. "Apparently this secret agency isn't so secret. They're... *officially* registered as a society of folklorists, down in Appalachia."

"Huh." John leaned in, reading. "Okay..." He scrolled through Becci's notes and clicked links, scanning interviews, blog posts, and even clips of television appearances made by some of the agents. *"Hiding in plain sight,"* John murmured.

"Exactly."

The earliest article detailed the founding of the group, first dubbed the *Cryptozoological Intelligence Center of America,* before it was truncated to a snappier name.

John patted the Cryptolabe. "So, what's this?"

Becci sighed and opened another tab.

"What?"

She rotated her laptop. "Press play."

John clicked.

"Now available at your local toyshop, it's the official CRYPTICA Paranormal Research Kit!" a rambunctious narrator proclaimed, as wild, 90's effects flashed over the screen and three excited kids cheered.

John sat back. "Oh, no way —"

"Keep watching."

One of the kids drew a plastic replica of the navigational tool, gasping as its bulbs lit up and oversized needle pointed to an action figure.

"It's a Chupacabra!"

"The K-field readings are off the charts!"

John frowned. *K-field?*

He was about to comment when Becci chimed, "*Keeeep* watching."

Electric guitar riffed over spooky sound effects while the kids snared the plastic monster with a toy net launcher and high-fived, suddenly dressed as mini men in black.

John started to laugh, but paused, when a baritone voice off-screen announced, "*Well done, agents,*" and the camera panned to a triad of serious-looking, suited gentlemen emerging from fog. John gaped at the middle one.

No way…

The figure's dark eyes squinted as he made a forced, half-smile, and the commercial cut to a close-up:

"*You, too, can uncover the truth,*" the tall, bald man spoke. On the lower left of the screen, he was accredited: *Giuseppe Scialpi, Agent of* CRYPTICA.

As the announcer's sped-up voice rattled off where the toy could be purchased, Becci tapped the pause button, and John slumped back in the booth.

His mind swirled and emotions cycled. First, he felt his neck muscles tighten, as Milly Matterhorn's catchphrase, *Redirection*, resurfaced in his memory.

CRYPTICA was employing a healthy dose of theater to keep the true extent of their research veiled. Next, he felt relief. It was a good thing Winslow had dissuaded them from mentioning the agents by name in the Giganteus story, John surmised. They were already on troubled waters with Nell, and an internet search yielding little more than a playful franchise would surely provide ample ammo for him to sabotage their credibility.

"Uh…" John managed to rasp after a moment. He cleared his throat. "Wow."

"Yep," Becci finished her coffee. "We're gonna have a hard time not looking like conspiracy theorists."

"If we even move ahead with this one."

"What do you mean, '*if?*' "

John's face stretched. "Well, if they aren't from around here… it isn't exactly local."

"You sound like Nell."

John swallowed. "I'm not trying to. But I know that's the kind of detail he'd levy against us. Besides, since Giganteus, things went pretty quiet on that front, right?"

"Au contraire mon frère..." Becci slid a folder from her pile. "I pulled some police records." She pushed it his way. "Turns out Bayfielders have been seeing 'men in black' sneaking around late at night."

John's heart thudded. *They're still here...?* He snatched up the papers and read the transcripts.

Becci's eyes lit up with a devious twinkle. She leaned back with her hands behind her head. "So, what's a bunch of harmless bookworms from Appalachia doing poking around our Sea Bound Coast, hm?" She crossed her boots, resting her case.

She was right, John knew. This story was huge. But he could foresee a million ways it could blow up in their faces. He tried to come up with a more roundabout approach.

"We could interview witnesses," John thought aloud. "Pose the question. Maybe the agents'll leave if they know the public's catching on."

"We could... *Or,*" Becci grinned sharply and held up the Cryptolabe, "we could blow the lid off their whole operation!"

"An exposé?"

"*Now* you're getting it!"

"That's a dangerous story, Becci," John warned. Becci looked enlivened by the term, but John insisted, "They already know about us." His eyes drifted to the police call transcripts. "We may be painting bigger targets on our backs..."

Becci took the folder back, shrugging. "They started it."

Tales from the Trident

ack in the day, I was a deckhand. A young boy on a mighty sailin' ship called the *Trident*," the old fisherman said, bulging, right eye glittering. "Most the crew was German. I thinks the Skipper hired me on account o' me name, or the fact that I was stronger'n I looked, n' none too picky 'bout the work I could get..."

"No shame in good honest work," one of the new regulars of Keeley's Bayside Eatery, a short, brawny, dark-haired man named Barnaby Smithins, commented between slurps of spiced cider, before plunking down his empty mug. "Speaking o' which..." He patted the counter. "Ken! I'm dying o' thirst out 'ere!"

"Yer an endless well!" Ken Keeley gruffed, returning from the kitchen to refill Barnaby's drink.

"There. Now, do me a favor n' actually *taste* this one. Ye camel." He marched off.

Barnaby's belly jiggled as he laughed, snapping his suspenders. "I'm just conditioning youse for the lunch rush, Ken. You're short-staffed, after all."

He was right. Muirin was out of town for the day, and Ken would have to tend to the masses on his own. That alone would be a tall enough order, notwithstanding the influx of townsfolk he suspected might track Winslow down to his establishment, especially given the latest fantastical tale that was slated to release today in the Bayfield Messenger. Ken swallowed hard.

"You're gettin' too popular for your own good! Why don'tcha hire more staff; make your life easy, eh?" Barnaby turned back to Winslow. "So, what were you saying about this *Trident?*"

"Yes..." Ken paled and hurried to the kitchen to prep. "Whatever tales are in ye, get 'em out o' yer system, quick!"

Winslow twinkled. "Whatever ya say, Keel." He swiveled to the small audience of Bayfielders in the otherwise empty eatery, all of whom looked honored and raring to hear an exclusive tale from the local legend.

"What *amazin' creature* is on your mind today?" Barnaby asked.

Winslow glanced at the rowboat painting on the far wall and smiled. "Anna."

Sal "Sleepy" Hurly arose from his rest on the counter, brown beard half-flat from his nap. "*The Anna?*"

"That's right. At this time in me life I hadn't met her yet. Circumstances was linin' up ta make that happen, though. Took me halfway 'cross the globe. But, when somethin's meant ta be, no distance is too great. 'Specially when yer aboard a great craft like the Trident...

"Our ship was a fine, antique vessel, y'see. A relic o' the golden age o' sailin'. So, when we came ashore, everyone knew it. We was gainin' a bit o' popularity among the local seasiders. Musta took us t'be a dashin' band o' foreign rogues. At least, that's what me ol' pal Kabel used ta say, n' he sure weren't 'bout ta correct 'em. 'Specially the lasses."

Winslow shook his head and sipped his root beer. "I swear, every time I looked right, that man was chattin' up a new girl up at the pub, braggin' 'bout his *Viking heritage* n' pointin' out his Norse tattoos. He even had the ship's namesake inked on his chest in bright blue. Said it showed the Skipper his devotion ta the rig." Winslow sniffed. "I thinks he just wanted another excuse ta take his shirt off."

Another newer patron, a woman with frizzed, honey-colored hair and a smoke-rasped voice named Reba Belle-Isle, fanned herself with the lapel of her leather jacket. "This *Kabel* friend of yours still around?"

Winslow huffed. "If he is, he'd be like..." He tried to do the math. "Eh... *old*." He laughed.

"Fine by me."

Barnaby chortled, "Ken! Reba needs a refill too. She's thirstier than me!"

"Anywho," Winslow grinned. "Turns out there was a girl at one o' these pubs that none had ever wooed. A girl named Anna Meria Lough. Didn't realize she had that reputation when I was talkin' ta her, though—tellin' her tales all night..."

" 'Bout monsters?" Ken called from the kitchen.

"Naw." Winslow shook his head. "Weren't none ta speak of quite yet."

The small audience gasped, hardly believing there was *ever* a time in Winslow Hoffner's life when he wasn't sharing stories of mythical beasts.

"I'm serious!" Winslow testified. "Won 'er over on me own merits, believe it or not. 'Parently the rest o' the Trident's crew was bettin' against me success in the corner o' the pub the whole time, though. 'Cept fer Kabel." Winslow slurped. "I think that's the day Kabel called me his best friend fer the first time. Since then, he declared himself me *wingman.*"

The fisherman's gaze strayed out the window, toward the clouds. "I thinks the full moon mighta had me back too that night, 'cause she kept the sky aglow with this gorgeous, celestial blue color, n' me n' Anna stayed up the whole time tradin' tales n' laughs. N' finally, our first kiss."

"*Aw,*" Reba crooned.

"Adda man!" Sleepy burbled.

Winslow shimmered at the memory. "Aye. So, every time we made port in that li'l Scottish harbor town, I'd stop by that seaside pub n' try ta see her."

"*Sea* her?" Sleepy smiled.

"Aye, Sleepy, sure."

"*Shore?*"

"Quit interruptin' the man!" Barnaby roared.

"Sorry."

"S'fine," Winslow chuckled. "Anywho, things were goin' great, till I realized just how smitten I was. Nerves gots the better o' me then. N' *then*, me *wingman* jumped in ta help:

" 'Say no more, *Kamerad*,' he boomed. 'Next we dock we'll pull out all the stops!'

"It got in me head that I needed new duds. Maybe it was 'cause Kabel was in me ear all the time sayin' I looked like a '*mangy sea dog*.'

"I said, 'Ain't that what we are?'

"N' he said, 'Ja, but you don't have to *look* like it!'

"He could tell I was as desperate as me fashion sense, so he let me in on a '*side hustle*' he said could get me some extra scratch fast so's I could impress me sweetheart. All I had ta do was help 'im move a few particular crates that night, n' not ask any questions.

"I said, 'What's so special 'bout these crates?'

"N' he said, 'That's a question.' "

The stare of the small audience deepened, some captivated, others confounded. This story was unlike most of the tales the fisherman was known to tell. No monsters had sprung from the deep yet, and some looked like they were becoming anxious awaiting the inevitable reveal of some mythical wonder. But for others, it was a rare look into the life of the enigmatic old man they'd come to find so fascinating. Nonetheless, all leaned in, as Winslow detailed a mysterious endeavor on the shore of Conwy, Wales:

"I was feelin' a little odd about the whole situation. But the next port we'd make after this'd be Anna's, n' I wanted ta show her I was more than a *sea dog*. We docked at Conwy n' did our usual errands." Winslow shook his head. "I tells ya, between our antique ship on that old pier n' the castles on them Arthurian shores, I felt like we'd sailed ourselves back in time..." He squinted, as the clouds outside the square window swirled like portals. His eye glimmered. "Midnight hit. N' Kabel n' me lugged this big, heavy crate outta the hold n' onta the pier. This crate was different from our normal cargo fer sure..."

"How so?" Reba asked.

"Well, fer one thing it was *growlin'!* Inside, I couldn't see nothin' but shadow, though, no matter how hard I looked. Kabel kept tellin' me it was fine, but I still had this naggin' feelin' tellin' me what we was doin' weren't right. I shoulda listened..."

The rolling waves and whistling wind painted the memory vividly. Winslow's stare went blank for a moment, before he took a shaky, steadying breath and continued:

"But, I traded the critter in the crate fer a few extra bucks. Kabel was all smiles. I was wrecked. Stayed up all night thinkin' 'bout the sound the poor animal made as it rolled off ta *who-knows-where.* Didn't help that every moan o' the ship sounded like one o' the crate critter's whimpers too..." Winslow's eye twitched. "Maybe they *were* whimpers, who knows. Kabel was dressin' nicer n' nicer every voyage, after all."

Winslow's throat bobbed as he took a slow sip and shook his head. "When we docked at Anna's port, me *wingman* dragged me all around town ta get me lookin' *'männlich'* enough fer me date. Spent every cent I had on this scratchy, gray suit that didn't even fit right. N' when I finally made it ta the pub, I didn't see no sign o' her…

"Afore I knew it, the Trident was shovin' off again. Fully stocked with cargo n' more o' Kabel's *specialty crates*, no doubt. N' I was just an overdressed fool swabbin' the deck.

"It was a while afore I gots me second shot with Anna. Thankfully it was right after I stopped listenin' ta Kabel, n' after that scratchy suit had worn some n' looked no different than me other rags. Anna said she liked her a scallywag."

Winslow smiled at the rowboat painting again, the waves rushing just beyond its wall seeming to give motion to the ripples on its peaceful lake. "Moral is, don't go changin' yerself fer someone. 'Specially since ya may end up changin' the thing that person likes the most!"

"N' when things're meant to be, they'll happen, if ya let 'em!" Sleepy added.

"Aye, Sleepy, that's a fair take too."

"What about the crate?" Barnaby asked.

"Hm?"

"The growlin' crate! Did you ever find out what was inside?"

Winslow swallowed.

Barnaby's eyes flashed. "Was it a *monster?*"

Reba sauntered by. "Not *every* story has to have a monster in it, Barn." She put her glass on the counter. Ken refilled it, keeping one wary eye on the new customers filing in, then snatching menus. As he rounded the corner, Reba put her elbow on the wall and dragged her finger along the anchor tattoo on Ken's forearm. "Nothing wrong with a little *love story*, eh, Ken?" She winked a few times.

Ken frowned. "What's wrong with your eye?"

"I'm winking."

"What for?"

Reba's head fell sideways. "I like to wink at clueless people."

"*What?*"

Reba sighed, as the harried man went to seat the restaurant's new arrivals, some of whom were whispering and pointing to the fisherman.

"*T'night's gonna be bonkers…*" Ken panted. As he passed by his friend's seat, he whispered, "*Say, I've a thought. Maybe if ye keep 'em distracted with more o' yer tales, n' I keep 'em drunk on two-dollar cider, they won't overload me kitchen. Keep 'em appeased, will ye?*"

"I was… thinkin' o' headin' back, actually—"

As Ken rushed by, Reba said, "*I* wouldn't mind hearing another love story."

"Not before a new *monster* story!" Barnaby said, with an echo of support. He started to say something more, but a mystical whistling in the wallboards and an odd spiral in the clouds beyond the window drew Winslow's attention back outside. The gray-blue overcast was warping and swirling in a pattern not unlike the misty skies of Conwy, and he felt a chill from the past creep up his neck.

"Care to tell us *exactly* vat happened here, Hoffner?" the graveled bark of Skipper Clint Horn demanded.

In German, the crew of the Trident muttered to one another around the gaping holes in the deck of the antique sailing ship. Bumping through the crowds, a blond, tattooed giant stopped before the damages, electric blue eyes peering through. Sea breezes whistled hauntingly through the dark fractures, and at a certain angle, a hidden stack of unmarked crates was just barely visible. For a moment, he thought he caught eyeshine peering back at him with a low growl through the shade, and he swiftly dragged boards over the rupture.

"Keep zat safe from zee elements, ja?" Tobias Kabel instructed, rubbing his huge hands. He then clopped over to his shaking friend and knelt by him. "Winslow, vat happened?"

The young deckhand shivered behind a splintered mess of overturned boxes and debris. In the low, dull glow of amber lanternlight, his eyes shined with fear. "Ya'd never believe it."

The handle of a lantern stretched with strings of goo as Kabel unhooked it, grumbling in disgust. The metal clanged and ooze rolled as it was set in the center of the ring of seafarers gathered around its light, while Winslow sat with a threadbare blanket over his shoulders. He nodded in thanks to a fellow crewman who brought him a steaming drink in a wooden cup.

Skipper uncorked a flask with his teeth, spat the cap, then gulped, burgundy juices drizzling over his strawy, white beard as his harsh eyebrows rested low on his icy stare. "*Venever* you're ready."

Winslow shivered, steam twirling by his spooked, pale features. "Thought at first me eyes was foolin' me," the young man finally began in a shaky whisper. "I was down in me cabin afore it happened, spent most the time lyin' in me hammock, pacin', or thinkin'. Ta be honest, I ain't been feelin' meself lately. That's why I asked ta stay aboard again... haven't been sleepin' right n' I didn't feel much like partyin'. So at first, I chalked up what I saw next ta tiredness..."

Kabel's tattooed chest rose and fell as he checked the quiet faces of the half-drunk crew, then steadied on the storyteller.

Winslow's eye bulged. "I saw me shadow on the wall. It looked... blurry, so I blinked. But it still didn't look right. It was... *shimmerin'*." The steam of his drink wisped and parted around the young man's eyes, darting as he retraced the image in the air and relived the experience. "I tracked the shape n' saw it didn't connect t'me. It..." He shuddered. "It stretched outta the open porthole. Some *nightmare* had slithered up the boat n' stuck ta the wall—*oozin'* n' *gushin'*—!"

"Hoffner is scared of his own shadow," one of the crewmen snickered.

Winslow straightened up. "Take a look around! Ya think a shadow can do *this?!*" he gritted, arm trembling at the dripping debris around him.

The man eased, as Winslow shook his head. "Ain't no shadow. I realized that soon as the thing sprouted these... horn-shaped things, n' a wigglin' beard o' feelers too, then peeled offa the wall, n' lunged fer me!" Winslow jolted. "I got outta the way just in the nick o' time, afore the creature ripped a clean hole in the deck like it was nothin'!"

Skipper sloshed his flask. "I'm not drunk enough for zis."

"I'm tellin' the truth! The horns on its head opened up with these li'l eyes that looked right at me."

"Eye stalks... like a slug?" Kabel asked.

"Aye, I guess."

Kabel nodded. The rest laughed.

Winslow threw down the blanket. "Yuck it up, fine! But listen here... it was the size o' this craft! N' it was takin' chunks outta the deck like it was made o' paper. It may've been a mollusk but it had teeth like a great white! When its head peeled back, all I could see inside was rings n' rings o' grindin' fangs! *RAAAH!*" he roared, taking the crew off-guard. Some flinched, others screamed, and one drunkenly fell off his seat.

Winslow's stare swept them, as the cold wisped through. "Yeah…" He walked. "Can't handle that? Imagine comin' face-ta-face with the teeth o' that *shadow*, chompin' floorboards ta bits!"

Winslow marched. The crew was silent. "The floor was disappearin' below me, so I had ta swing from the hammocks. Fer some reason it squeezed back out the porthole, so I clapped it shut. But the weight o' this… *thing* was pressin' hard on the ship, tiltin' 'er. Walls became floors fer a second, n' I scrambled sideways till I got topside. That's when I finally got a good look:

"Pitch-dark n' shimmerin' like a livin' night sky. Ribbony wigglers flowin' down either side o' the flat of its tummy, with flappin' paddlers on its chest that sucked ta the hull. On her back was this big ol' rock-colored shell that was bendier than ya'd think, n' its tailfin looked like a soggy flag."

Some of the crewmen were swayed by the specificity and certainty of the account. Others argued the impossibility of such a beast. Winslow was firm, but a growing swell of rebuff began to drown him out, until Kabel boomed:

"I believe him!" He stood, huge chest puffed with blue, Norse filigree, as his matching eyes struck the sailors. "In Cornwall I heard tell of such a myth. Zey call it zee *Morgawr*." The tines of his trident tattoo rose sharply from his collar. "I believe our great Trident vas attacked. Und Winslow Hoffner saved us from shipwreck!"

Heads turned, amazed. Skipper finished off his flask. "*Now* I'm drunk enough." He wobbled, and burped. "Go on, Hoffner. How'd you fend off zee *Mor-gog-gull?*"

In the glow of the lantern, Winslow's face was lit with gold. "Weren't easy," he said. "The deck was nearly sideways again, n' slicked with slime, but I grabbed whatever I could ta fence the thing back. Boards, mops, ya name it! But every time that toothy maw just grinded 'em all inta sawdust!"

The crew whispered, becoming convinced the lines of slime that webbed their ship and the mess of damage left behind was indeed the aftermath of a phantasmagoric duel between man and monster.

"I was hangin' onta the rail as it gnashed. Despite me best efforts it nabbed a chunk o' me jacket, n' a chunk o' the deck too."

Kabel vouched, "Now you *know* zee man's truthful. Zat's zee only nice clothes he has!"

The crew nodded, convinced by *that* detail more than anything.

Winslow let the comment slide. "That beast woulda done more damage had one o' Skipper's barrels not plugged the way. When its teeth came down, n' the contents gushed inta its mouth, I saw the—" He looked to Kabel. "Morgawr?" At a nod, he continued, "—toss n' wobble, then it got all confused n' turned 'round, splashin' ta the abyss in a spiral." Winslow breathed. "Never seen anythin' like it."

"Morgawr got *beschwipst* on Skipper's sauce! *Ha!*" one sailor rejoiced, while Skipper panicked and staggered. "Zis calls for a celebration!"

Skipper stood by his busted barrel, burgundy juice dribbling. "Vith *vat*?" he lamented.

Winslow blinked at the boards lying over the hole in the deck. "Kept goin' fer that same spot…" The innards of the ship rumbled and moaned. "Maybe it weren't after me after all…"

Kabel blocked the young deckhand's view and wrapped his shoulders with a huge, inked arm. "Zis man's a hero! He should be treated as such!"

"*Ja!*" the Trident's crew cheered.

"Er ist der *König der Biester*, ja?"

"*Ja!*"

"Wunderbar." Kabel patted Winslow and brought him along, telling Skipper they'd pick up supplies for the ship from town.

"Forget zee supplies, get spirits!" Skipper bawled, as the two men disembarked.

Squeaking over the sodden pier while the Trident's crew cleared muck and kept wary eyes on the waters, Kabel guided his friend into Conwy's towns, passing castles that heralded their entrance, and clopping into a serene village.

"Thanks fer havin' me back, Kabel."

"Vat're *vingmen* for? Sanks for not mentioning zee *special cargo*. Vee have another delivery tonight, if you're up for it."

"Yeah… count me outta that one, will ya?"

"You sure? Fast cash."

"Yeah," Winslow winced. "Don't think yer guys are too fond o' me since the incident last time."

"Oh, vee vere *both* to blame for zat, Kamerad. Loose ropes. Zee cargo escaped. It happens."

"Right."

"*Und* you chased zee little scamp for quite some time before it got avay."

Winslow swallowed. "Right."

Kabel made a thoughtful frown, then shook his friend's shoulders. "Vant a drink?"

"Ain't thirsty." Winslow pulled on his shredded jacket, then changed the subject. "Quite the speech ya gave back there, Kabel. *'Our great Trident…'* Almost forgot how bad ya wanted offa that rig."

Kabel palmed the trident tattoo on his chest. "Zee best vay to *get along* is to *go along*, ja? Zat's zee difference between you und me, Kamerad." His electric blue eyes sparkled. "You're a *terrible* liar."

Winslow frowned, and before he could ask what he meant, a huge hand came down on his shoulder.

Someone shook him. "What was in the crates, eh?"

"Huh?"

Suddenly back in the present, Barnaby pressed, "The crates, Wins! You said one was *growlin'*! That's a monster story in the makin' if I ever heard one. Will you tell us?"

Winslow glanced around Keeley's Bayside Eatery, as his listeners grinned, eager. The fisherman managed to return a smile and say, "Maybe later."

The group groaned a little but accepted the answer, excited conversations blending into a hum. Winslow's throat clenched and eye twitched, feeling icy drafts howl against his back, as more patrons pushed through the old doors behind him.

Troubled Waters

old wind sliced the clemency. Anna Meria Lough shivered and clutched her shoulders.

"No worries, hun, I'll get'cha back," her sailor assured her.

Anna's sea-blue eyes welled with worry, as a foggy chatter slipped through her lips. The young Winslow Hoffner pulled off his coat and draped her, then got back into rowing position and plied the oars. But the shore only stretched farther the more he pulled. He checked over his shoulder at the mist that crept over their lake, hiding the blue. He grunted. When his lady spoke his name, it echoed apart, distant, disappearing. And when he raised his head to answer her, she had vanished.

"Anna?" He stood and turned. The empty, wooden rowboat rocked. The fog was constricting now, all-encompassing, save for a small portal where a lone willow swayed on the dark bank. "ANNA!"

He went to cup his hands around his mouth and call again, but discovered they were suddenly bound behind him. He tugged in horror and felt the dig of ties on his wrists, then a flash of pain across the back of his head.

His knees buckled and knocked hard into the ringing floor, metal now. A different boat in a different time. Another lake, swathed in mist and spotlit in the dull, haunting rays of a blood moon. And more chilling than the cruel winds that howled on his raw, beaten skin was the click of a cocking gun behind him, and the voice of its shadowy holder:

"Where do you think you are, Mr. Hoffner?"

The glint of metal poised like a hungry predator. A finger touched the trigger.

SNAP!

"Wins!" Ken snapped his fingers.

Winslow shook free, back at Keeley's Bayside Eatery, vision stretching from the rowboat painting on the far wall. He had gotten lost in his own mind again. "What?" he murmured. "What was that?"

"You tell me!" Ken's red eyebrows wiggled over his distraught stare. "Yer freakin' me out, friend. Ye keep dazin' off. Have ye been to a doctor of late?"

"Aw, Keel, I'm fine —"

"I'm serious, Wins."

"I'm just thirsty is all."

Ken relented and made him a glass of his signature drink, tracing the fisherman's stolid stare to his painting.

"Yer gonna make off with more o' me art? Is that it? Are ye plannin' a heist?"

Winslow managed a smile. "Naw." His fingers squeezed the handle of the glass mug, knuckles white. "Just gots a bit on me mind."

"Ye want to talk about it?"

"Think I'm gonna get a breath actually." Winslow pushed off the counter with a grunt and hobbled down the hall with his soda, passing the painting and pushing through a stiff side door leading to an outdoor seating area on a miniature, pier-like deck. He faced the roaring swirls of the bay and sat, wind making a grim whistle as a wreath made of a dried shark jaw clacked on the glass, and the door hissed shut.

Ken swallowed. "Hm."

WHUMP! The cook jumped when heavy stacks of papers came down on the counter.

"Jesus, lad!"

A lanky, nervous-looking young man's tired arms hung loosely on the sides of his delivery. "They were heavy," he shivered an apology to the broad-shouldered cook.

Behind him, another man strolled up casually, one hand in the pocket of his gray overcoat, the other holding a steamy cup of lavender tea under his confident smile. "There now, Len. We'll have to build up your upper body strength, won't we?"

The new intern, Lenny Quint, panted bashfully as his boss stepped around him and offered a hand to Ken. "I'm not sure we've met. Nell Dunney, assistant editor at the Messenger."

"Ah," Ken grunted, arms folded.

An unreturned handshake turned into a pat on the bar counter. "Fine establishment you have here. I'm assuming you're Keeley?"

"The second."

"Family business! What a treat," Nell crooned. "We won't be long. I was just showing young Len here the ropes as we make the rounds with our latest issue. I imagine you're excited since word around town is this," he palmed the front page of the top of the stack, "*man of the sea* is a regular of yours."

"He's my supplier."

"He around?"

Ken glanced out the rectangular, glass window of the side door, seeing the fisherman sitting quietly on the breezy deck. "I don't think he's up for another interview."

"Oh, nothing of that sort. Just a quick hello."

Ken rotated a toothpick in his teeth, checked his friend again, then tightened his crossed arms, anchor tattoo on his forearm bulging and making Lenny gulp. He lifted his chin to the tea in Nell's hand. "No outside food or drink, by the way."

Nell read the cook's face, then set his drink loosely on the edge of the counter. "Len, be a sport and pop that in the bin for me."

As Lenny went to take it, Nell released the cup early and it flipped, splashing onto the floor. The intern spluttered apologies while Ken grumbled curses and went for a rag. Nell slipped through the side door.

Squawks of lonely gulls and the clang of a brassy wind chime accompanied the chilly timbre of gales, as rolling waves thrummed under it all. Winslow breathed in the solitude a moment longer, squinting into the distance, until the clops and squeaks of footsteps on boards drew near, and the chair beside his made a metallic whine.

"It's Winslow, isn't it?"

Winslow sipped his root beer.

"I don't know if you remember me. You and I had a brief," Nell's smile flickered with wolfish scorn, then concealed, "*run-in* at the Messenger. I'm one of the editors there. I've been publishing your little fables."

Winslow stared ahead, chest rising and falling with the waves.

"Dreaming up the next one?" Nell traced his gaze, seeing nothing. "Your friend at the bar says you're feeling a tad under the weather. What's troubling you? Stress?" Nell checked for changes in the fisherman's face. "Guilt?" When Winslow still said nothing, Nell's cheer faded. His coaly eyes burned.

"Well, whatever's eating you, just know this..." He stood, his hand on the back of the old man's chair, and smiled. "You *deserve* it."

The side door squealed open. "Exit's out front," Ken called.

Nell swiveled, happy, sniffing the brine and nodding at the creeping gray above. "Best we get a move on." He snaked around the cook and patted Lenny's shoulder, who wheezed under the final stack of papers. "Just one stop to go."

Ken watched them leave, then edged closer to his friend. "That gobshite give ye trouble?"

Winslow's stare deepened on the bay, its swirls portaling him into fiercer memories. Haunting figures, cold metal gleaming in moonlight, flashes of white fangs in black waters, then red in those waters.

"He ain't nothin'."

John Chaplain and Becci Hamrin plugged away at their research, compiling findings, jotting interview questions, and sharing punchy laughs, before revivifying their spirits and focus with sips of fresh coffee, which the barista, Winter, was quick to provide.

Winter's cheeks buzzed as she filled John's cup. "I may have to cut you off soon."

"I can handle it."

Winter giggled and slipped away.

Becci rolled her eyes.

John laughed, "What?"

"She's practically draping herself over the table and singing you show tunes now."

"Oh, c'mon." John scratched the back of his head. "What, you think I should ask her out?"

Becci picked at a muffin, squinting in thought, and popped a blueberry-dotted clump in her mouth. Before she could answer, the latest issue of the Bayfield Messenger appeared between them, offered by the new intern.

"Delivery." Lenny handed John and Becci each copies and rubbed his sore shoulder, then smoothed his frizzed, black hair. "Extra, extra." He laughed quietly.

"Thanks, Lenard," Becci said. "It's Lenard right? Or Lenny?"

"Uh, either works. Lenny's good."

"Finally a little downtime, eh, Len?"

"Or that."

Nell strolled up, clapping the tall, young man's shoulder. "How's about lunch? Pick whatever you like, mate."

"Thanks, Mr. Dunney."

"Anytime, sport. Ask Winter for the usual for me."

John and Becci tensed.

"Good kid." Nell gestured to the intern. "You two look like you're keeping diligent. That's good."

"*Yep*," John and Becci said at the same time.

Nell snickered, "Oh, that was *cute*."

"Nell Dunney? Is that our favorite poet?"

"Ah, my reputation precedes me." He caught Winter in a hug.

John swallowed. *Of course*, he thought, then cringed at the image of Nell delivering poetry. Judging from Becci's expression, she was similarly shocked, but trying to keep from laughing instead.

Nell eyed them, then switched back to Winter as she asked, "Open mic's tonight. Did you bring any new poems?"

"Not on me, but bring me a few napkins and I can scrawl something up."

"So talented," Winter sang. She looked at John and Becci. "Are you two staying a little longer?"

"Uh…"

"Nope," Becci answered for both of them, straightening up their work.

John agreed, "Yeah. Rain check."

Winter drained a little. "Oh. Okay. It was, um, good meeting you." She shook their hands and waved, getting back to her station.

"Meeting your fisherman friend again at that fish bar?" Nell asked.

John pulled a satchel over his shoulder, while a blender whirred behind the counter.

"Ah, well. Maybe we'll catch each other at the next open mic." With Winter and Lenny gone, Nell leaned in. "You two could participate! Bring one of your articles to read." He winked. "Next weekend is *flash fiction* night."

John and Becci left.

"Mr. Dunney," Lenny said, bringing his boss' drink over.

Nell held out his hand to receive the fresh, mixed-berry smoothie. He watched the journalists exit as he slurped the red slush.

"How is it?" Winter asked.

His tongue snapped as he gave a satisfied, stained grin. "Sweet."

The door chimed and clattered as John and Becci plodded down the chilly sidewalk.

"Well, that place is ruined forever," John shivered.

Becci giggled. "I dunno. It may be worth it to hear *Mr. Dunney's* poetry sometime." She fawned, posing Shakespearianly, "*Hark!* If only I were as good a writer as John Chaplain!"

John laughed.

"*Hark!* I'm not fooling anyone with this hair dye!"

A tap on John's shoulder made the two turn. It was Winter. Becci's cheeks puffed as she halted her theatrics, but the barista didn't seem to have heard.

She smiled, giving John a to-go cup. "One for the road."

John thanked her, and she trotted back inside. He turned the cup around to see a phone number was written on the side in black marker. He flushed. "Huh."

Becci's brow arched. "Told ya. You were putting out the vibe."

"I guess you know me better than I know myself."

Becci pushed her hands into the pockets of her puffy, purple jacket. "So?"

"What?"

"You gonna text her?"

"Well…" John swallowed, then shrugged. "She doesn't know me. *And* she's a friend of Nell's."

Becci's olivine eyes flicked between John's thoughtful face and the number on the cup. She sighed. "She's an *acquaintance* with who Nell *pretends* to be," Becci clarified. "You're honest. So, technically, she knows you better than she ever knew him." She tapped the coffee in her friend's hand. "And if you ask me, she's got good taste."

A clattering din came from the kitchen as Ken rifled to fill orders. The floors were packed, stuffed to the brim with patrons clutching copies of the latest issue of the Bayfield Messenger, and hoping to hear more stories from the man himself.

Winslow sat stoically at his usual spot, zoning out on occasion, but drifting back at the excited requests of the townsfolk:

"Have ye any new stories, Wins?"

"Ever find out what the mystery whale was?"

"Glum night out there, ain't it? How's about a *scary* story?"

Winslow caught the last question. "Scary, eh? Let's see…" He rubbed his chin, grinning. "Once, I met a man named Keeley."

The crowd laughed.

"I heard that!" Ken barked. He came out of the kitchen with arms full of plates, eyeing Winslow, who chuckled a little before turning pensive again. Ken shook his head and hollered, "Comin' through," as he navigated. Neither as small nor as speedy as Muirin, he bumped, squeezed, and grunted through the packed restaurant, just barely managing to keep the place fed. He looked forward to his mother's return from her trip.

Ken dabbed his forehead and muttered to himself, *"Alright, drinks."*

The crowd huzzahed.

The uproar quaked him. Over the noise, he asked his friend, "Are ye gonna give these folks a scary story? 'Cause they're scarin' *me!*"

Sleepy patted Winslow's back. "Ah, but what could poss'bly scare the great Winslow Hoffner, eh?"

Winslow sank into the rowboat picture on the far wall again, blinking slowly, as his root beer hovered, fizzing under his lips. "Scariest thing in the world is underestimatin' mother nature."

Ken's eyes tightened at his friend's grim tone, but Sleepy hooted, "*Ooh-hoo!* Now *that's* what I call settin' the scene!" before returning to his doze on the counter.

The shapes of John and Becci appeared in the windows of the entrance. In Becci's hands the paper was fanned, finishing a cursory glance at the final version of their story.

"Yeah, Nell really knows how to suck the punch out of a piece," she said, flipping back to the new headline, *Alleged Sighting of 'Mystery Whale' in Bay, Local Fisherman Claims 'Monsters Are Real.'*

"A rose by any other name," John reminded her. "I was expecting worse, honestly. I think Albert softened the blow. Plus, all the quotes are really strong."

The journalists were barely able to fit in the door. Ahead, a sea of Bayfielders were hoisting their own copies and eagerly squeezing in to listen to the fisherman at the bar.

"I guess they did the trick?" Becci murmured.

John agreed, stunned by the volume. He tried to call at Winslow, but was shushed by one of the patrons, as the fisherman dredged through memories and mumbled a yet-unshared tale, less bombastic than usual.

Is he okay? John wondered. He and Becci missed the opening but leaned in to listen as best they could:

"I was bein'…" Winslow's eye twitched. He rubbed his wrists. *"Ehm…* escorted… by a few folks that was chasin' the beasties that'd run off ta make their home in a spot called Misty Lake."

"What'd you say the creatures were again?" Linda Cunningham asked.

"Most of 'em were yer standard Icelandic Sea Wolves n' Irish Crocodiles."

The crowd giggled at the novelty of the names, and Peter Matterhorn took a break from his plate of saucy chicken wings to say, "I've never heard *this* one." He licked his thumb. "Icelandic Sea Wolves. Was this in Iceland then?"

"Naw."

"Ireland?"

"Naw. Wales."

"*Whales* in a *lake?*" Sleepy burbled, awake.

"Naw, the lake was *in* Wales."

Barnaby Smithins nudged Sleepy with his elbow. "The whale was yesterday. The man jus' said they were wolves n' crocodiles for Pete's sake."

Peter joked, "No need to clarify for my sake, I was followin'."

The half-drunk audience groaned, but Sleepy guffawed. A grin tugged free on Winslow's face for a second, seeing the cheer of his friends. And when he caught sight of John and Becci near the entrance he gave a broader grin, picking up:

"Ta clarify, them critters' names was only *colloquial*, y'see. The 'crocodiles' was more like big angry otters, n' the 'wolves' was more like shelled, toothy water-weasels."

The audience lapped up the details, twinkles of discovery in their eyes.

"This sounds so *fake*," Ken chuckled. "Been a spell since I visited the motherland, but I nary heard tell of an *Irish Crocodile*."

"Well, I'm tellin' ya now. They's also called *Dobhar-chú*."

"Bless ya!" Sleepy said.

Winslow glanced at both of them. "*Anywho...*" His focus shifted, as headlight beams flashed through the front windows and stretched his listeners' shadows across the wall. Three shapes towered ominously. "These folks that wanted the critters... they got a li'l impatient when the beasties didn't show at first. They didn't like that. They thought maybe I was leadin' 'em astray this whole time..." Winslow shivered. "Truth is I *was* tryin' to. But we arrived all the same, like the woods had... just spat us out there."

"This is a bit intense," Ken cut in, wiping a glass, "What were ye doin' in Wales in the first place, friend? On holiday with Anna?"

Barnaby's eyes sparked. "Or was this from your time on the *Trident?*"

At the barrage of questions, Winslow went rigid. The shark jaw wreath on the side door cast a haunting shadow on the lake painting.

"*Um…*" Winslow's head pounded.

As he traced the shadow, the toothy wreath seemed to warp, serrated enamel sheening silver in moonlight. Winslow flinched at the snapping sound made by a cracking crab leg, and he covered his forehead, as the happy laughter around him blended into a single, sharp shriek.

Across the restaurant, John felt a pulse of horror. *Something's wrong.*

Becci felt it too. She traded concerned glances, then called Winslow's name.

"Sh!" a listener hushed her.

"You *sh!*" Becci snapped.

A little old woman paled.

Becci swallowed her outburst, then locked arms with John as they pushed their way to the front.

At the pause in the story, Ken, distracted, teased, "He's realizin' the details don't add up."

Wallboards warped with heavy gales, matching the howls of Misty Lake. Whether they were of wind, beast, or man Winslow still didn't know. He turned in his barstool, just as he'd turned to his captors in the crimson glow of the blood moon, on the cold metal of that silver boat, staring down atrocities.

The audience, invested, called out:

"What was it? An Irish Crocodile?"

"An Icelandic Sea Wolf?"

"*Somethin' else,*" Winslow managed to answer.

"A third monster, huh?" Ken let out a tickled laugh as he dunked fish sticks in a fryer.

Winslow plunged deeper into the memory of raging bubbles, fangs, screams, and gunshots. The fisherman's vision blurred as though underwater, and the painting of the rowboat seemed farther away than ever.

Peter broke a wingbone and a timer in the kitchen went off. Winslow's ears rang as John called his name again, and Ken swung out of the kitchen with a steaming plate.

"Ain't nothin' shameful 'bout bein' on a simple getaway with yer lass, Wins—"

CRASH!

The barstool flung out from behind the fisherman and clattered over the floor as he shot up, wet eyes locked on something invisible, fists tight.

The bar was silent.

John reached out. *"Winslow?"*

The fisherman took a few breaths into his shaking chest, saying nothing more, then left. His root beer, and the tale, went unfinished.

Ken looked shaken. He called out, "Wins! I-I was just bustin' yer chops, friend—!" But the exit thumped shut before he could finish. The restaurant murmured, as Ken repeated, "I *was just bustin' his chops...*"

John lowered into a seat, feeling a heaviness compress on him. *What happened?* As soon as the thought appeared, so did Muirin, trundling through the entrance and glancing into the night behind her.

"Oh." She touched her heart. "Poor man." She pulled off her fluffy hat. "It's always hard fer widowed folks like us on days like these."

"What days?" Ken asked.

Muirin, just noticing the tense spectators of her eatery and the worry in her son's eyes, unraveled her scarf. "Anniversaries," she explained shakily. "This week is Winslow and Anna's."

The room became even quieter. Ken sank. Muirin wrung her scarf, shuffling up to the bar and touching her son's arm.

"What's wrong?"

Ken sighed. "I wish ye'd been here to *poke* me before I said somethin' stupid."

Trunko

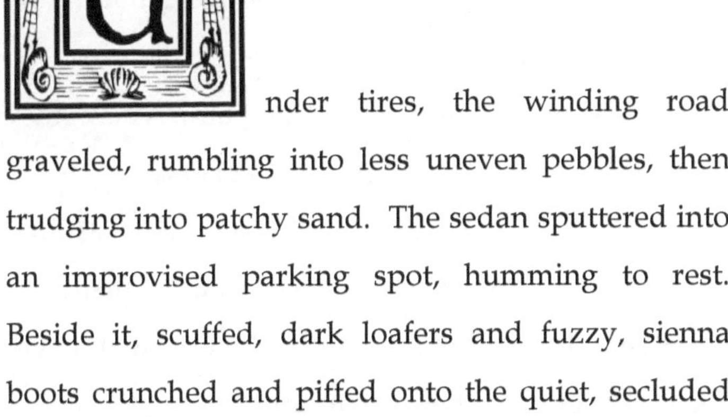nder tires, the winding road graveled, rumbling into less uneven pebbles, then trudging into patchy sand. The sedan sputtered into an improvised parking spot, humming to rest. Beside it, scuffed, dark loafers and fuzzy, sienna boots crunched and piffed onto the quiet, secluded beach, toward the subdued, fizzing waves of the shore and the square, floating home of Winslow Hoffner.

Back where he'd first interviewed the fisherman, John Chaplain breathed in the cool, afternoon vista. Unlike the torrential conditions of that first night, there was a cautious quiescence about it now. Nestled where the woodlands spilled into a sandy cove, the houseboat looked like a maritime cabin: ropey fencing on its porch, round lanterns swinging on its overhangs, and waterlogged, wooden walkways hugging its exterior and crossing onto a ramshackle pier, where the Seanna was docked, bobbing just slightly taller than the roof of the houseboat with which it shared harbor.

"Hope he's alright," John said.

Becci Hamrin gave him a reassuring nod. "He will be. C'mon."

They shuffled onto a central path, where they intersected with a second pair of trekkers.

"Oh, uh, hey there," Ken Keeley said, striding alongside his mother, who waved gently at them.

"Ken, Muirin, hey," John replied. He'd never seen them outside their restaurant.

"We was just... ehm, droppin' by to say—" He coughed, showing a case of root beer. "I mean... just to see how the ol' coot's doin', since... y'know."

"Same," Becci said.

Around the corner of the houseboat, they saw Winslow step out, just barely visible on his balcony. In his mouth, he trilled on the brass bosun pipe, and John's mind flashed, remembering the jaws of Gambo bursting from the tides to char and chaw the meal he tossed her.

Becci froze too. *"The whistle…"*

Ken frowned. "What whistle?"

Neither could reply. They were fixed on the bay, waiting. But after a few more notes, the waters remained still, popping, and the fisherman pocketed the odd instrument and ambled back in.

Ken looked the journalists over, sniffing. *"Ooookay,* then." He trudged on with Muirin. Becci hung back with John.

"What do you think Ken would've done if Gambo showed up?"

Probably the same as us, John mused, reliving how his body locked up at the sight of the legend, and the life-changing revelations thereafter. Maybe Ken would become a believer one day.

"She ain't showin'," Winslow mumbled, pacing.

"Give it time."

"This's the second time."

From his seat in the living room, Hank Malloy reclined, drumming a beer bottle. "Hm. Ye think she's moved on?"

"Don't know." Winslow's jaw fidgeted, eyes scanning the floorboards. "Things've been strange lately."

Hank chuffed, "Things're *always* strange."

"Aye. It's just... ever since the momma whale's eye opened on me, I ain't stopped... dreamin' 'bout the past."

"Good or bad?"

"Bit o' both. Mostly 'bout where it all began." He pivoted, gesturing to the empty waves lulling on the bay. "Now this... I ain't sayin' they's connected, but they feel like it t'me."

"Everythin's connected, Wins."

"Mm."

"An' if'n ye's feelin' a connection, maybe your soul's tryin' tae tell ye somethin'."

"I *feel* like there's somethin' I oughtta do..." Winslow ruminated. "Or somethin' I oughtta have done already. Just can't figure what."

"For now, all ye *have* tae do is go with the flow."

"I gots a hard time lettin' go, Hank."

Hank nodded to the menagerie of knickknacks and artifacts from the fisherman's adventures nailed to the walls and populating the shelves. He smiled at them, pieces of magic from all over the world. "I know," he said. "Yer a mighty sailor, Wins, but ye cannae change the wind. Listen for a while instead. Maybe then your answer will come a'knockin'."

Three knocks came at the door just then. The fishermen traded glances.

Hank's grin curled. "Damn, I'm good!"

The front door squeaked, and Ken, Muirin, John, and Becci gave overlapped hellos and well-wishes to Winslow. Surprised and honored, the fisherman waved them all in. Hank smiled from his seat, tipping his drink to them.

"Hey, Wins," Ken nodded. He rocked on his heels and glanced toward the balcony. "So, I hears yer takin' up music now."

"Nope."

"Oh..." He looked left again, frowning, then shook his head. "Right, um, anyways, this's for you."

"Ah, thanks Keel!" Winslow took the case of root beer. "What fer?"

"Peace offerin'. I wanted to apologize, for what happened the other night. I wasn't tryin' to..." He sighed. "I mean, I didn't know... about Anna—"

"S'fine, Keeley. It weren't you or anythin' ya said. It's just me—somethin' I'm tryin' ta figure out. I'm okay though." He patted the root beer case, smiling. "N' don't thinks ya ever needs a reason ta come by with one o' these."

Ken chuckled, relieved. "Alright, friend. Ye got it." They patted each other's backs, and Muirin shuffled up next, arms open.

"C'mere." They hugged.

"Thanks, Mrs. Keel. I just been thinkin' 'bout her is all. Thinkin' 'bout a lot o' things."

"The type o' love ye have in yer heart for that gell will keep her spirit beside ye, always."

Winslow nodded.

"N' ye *always* have family in the Keeleys!"

Winslow thanked her again as she pecked him on the cheek. John and Becci came in next with a double-hug, and the fisherman laughed a little through his nose as he caught them.

"Thanks fer comin'."

"Sure thing," John said.

"Anytime," Becci added.

In the living room, Winslow clicked on a heater in the shape of a freestanding, iron fireplace. The fake logs glowed with red, artificial flame.

"Cozy, eh?" he chuckled.

While the rest of the party settled into chairs, stools, and one torn, old couch, Becci moseyed by Winslow's shelves of curios, seeing his impressive collection for the first time. Ships in bottles, bobble-heads, carved wooden figures of sea creatures and sailors, and an overlapped showcase of photos galore — of a young Winslow in foreign lands, group photos of crews, friends sharing laughs, and a red-haired woman with a kind smile and daring, blue eyes.

"Is this Anna?" Becci asked, lifting one of the pictures of her and Winslow on a boat.

"Aye."

Becci smiled. "She's beautiful, Winslow."

Winslow nodded. "Aye."

"Where were you in that picture?" John asked, glimpsing the azure waves.

"South Africa."

Muirin twinkled. "Chasin' monsters?"

"Naw. Just enjoyin' ourselves," Winslow said, smiling dreamily at a memory, then adding, "But a monster did show up, o'course."

"O'*course*," Ken said.

Muirin elbowed him.

"I mean… oh *really?*"

Winslow noticed the change in Ken's pitch and snorted. "Ya prolly wouldn't want ta *hear* it though…"

Ken looked at his mother, then swallowed. "No, no, I'd love to hear it! Honest!"

"It's a *good'n*," Hank attested.

Winslow stroked his beard. "I dunno…"

"I won't question a word ye say, in fact!" Ken added.

Winslow's right eye sparkled, as though sensing a challenge.

Here we go, John thought, wondering how long Ken would be able to keep his promise.

"Alrighty, then!" Winslow got into a red chair by the fire. "Picture this—!" The photo was propped up beside him on an end table as Becci sat beside John on the couch. Winslow began:

"Anna n' me was out on a sightseein' excursion on this handsome boat called the *Pisces*, coaxed aboard with promises o' majestic seascapes n' killer whales! Little did we know we'd be gettin' a two-fer-one special!" He held up the picture. "This's us on the boat."

In the photo, Winslow sat against the guardrail. He was young—skinny still, but with some muscle, blond chest hair showing over his half-unbuttoned blue shirt. One arm rested high on the rail, the other embraced his wife. Anna, fair, sat to his right, her ruby locks flowing under a stylish, wide-brimmed sunhat, shoulders clad in a floaty, angelic, white shawl, with her legs crossed over her husband's lap.

"Couple o' heartthrobs, weren't we!"

The room agreed.

"Still are!" Muirin cooed.

Winslow chuckled. "Maybe we was too distracted with each other ta sense what was trailin' us. This was our first time off on a whirlwind adventure in the Indian Ocean t'gether." He set the photo down. "These certainly weren't me usual waters. N' I *certainly* weren't expectin' no monsters—"

"But fate had other plans!" Hank hurrahed.

"Aye, so it seemed. The greatest moments always pop up when ya least suspect 'em, I s'pose. 'Cause just then—!" He punched. "*KA-FLOOM!* Up came these spouts! Killer whales—two of 'em—were keepin' pace with our li'l vessel. Happened so fast the cap'n weren't even prepared. He started cheerin' o'er the speakers fer us ta look left. So we did. Thing is, there was more'n just orcas in the water..." Winslow's buggy, right eye flashed at Muirin. "We may not've been chasin' beasties that day, Mrs. Keel, but them *orcas* sure was!"

Muirin bounced. "What *was* it?"

"At the time, it weren't nothin' but a blur. Furry, flippery, n' fast."

"A seal?" John thought aloud, then shook his head. *This is Winslow. Of course it wasn't a seal.* But to his surprise, Winslow smiled and said:

"Ya ain't too far off, Chaplain. I thought the same at the time. N' if it'd stayed under, I may've thought that's *all* it was. That is, till I saw the creature's *strangest* feature."

"Did it breathe fire?" Ken harrumphed. He caught a glare from his mother, then swallowed. "Honest question!"

"Naw," Winslow chuckled. "Not this one."

"Was it *huge?*" Becci asked.

"This one weren't more'n a pup."

"Did it have *wings?*" Hank jumped in.

Winslow blinked. "Ya know it doesn't, ya've heard this'n."

"Aye, I just wanted tae participate."

"Ah," Winslow laughed. "Fair 'nough."

"What made it so strange, then?" John implored.

Winslow buzzed, "A trunk!" With his arm and hand, he imitated the motion of the long nose spraying from the waves and steadying like a submarine's periscope. "Anna n' me was shocked! Ain't never seen a sniffer like *this* on a critter like *that.*"

John stroked his chin, fascinated. Becci kicked her legs up on an ottoman and crossed her feet.

"Trunk, eh?" Ken said.

"Aye. His name was Trunko."

"Ah. Fittin'."

"Yep! N' when his li'l black eyes blinked upon our ride, the pup made this tootin' sound n' dove. Went paddlin' like mad right underneath us! Problem was, the orcas did too… They musta been real famished, 'cause they didn't mind boppin' our boat while they gave chase. The cap'n had a good start about it, fightin' with the wheel…"

Winslow imitated the captain's desperate stance, catching the helm. "He shouted, *'Eish! Hold on!'* n' we clutched the bars tight. Anna n' me weren't goin' nowhere, but that pup sure was. Couldn't see the sprout fer a spell, but we was rootin' fer 'im. Anna was callin' at the deep, her hand held out…"

Winslow blinked. In his mind he was there again. "That gal was the kindest-hearted woman I've ever known."

"And the feistiest!" Muirin added. "*Hoo!* Ye di'n't wanna be on 'er bad side!"

"Right! She looked like she was 'bout ta bare-knuckle brawl them orcas herself. Luckily fer the orcas, she didn't have ta, 'cause the pup came rocketin' skyward! Fer such a pudgy fella, he sure was spry."

Hank drummed his round belly. "We's can be quick when we wanna be. *Ha!*"

"Near-death experiences are a good motivator too," Becci said.

"Aye. Anna even managed ta unchain n' swing open the bar at the back o' the boat just in time. When the pup flopped aboard, we finally got us a good look at 'im. Looked like an elephant seal that took the 'elephant' part too literal."

The room chuckled.

Winslow went on, "It was covered in white fuzz like an *arctic* seal, though. Real fluffy." Winslow searched the ceiling and grinned, touching his brow. "Yeah, I remember he had these li'l gray spots 'round one eye, like daisy petals. N' his back flipper had these odd platy parts—not like a shell exactly, but segmented in a *foldy* way, enough ta look like a lobster's tail."

Muirin covered her heart at the sweet and whimsical description. Ken's face was turning bright red. He surely had a million discrepancies that he wanted to highlight, but he held them all in. Hank was holding his head.

"*Oooh,*" the first mate groaned. "Every time ye say *lobster* I get dizzy, Wins."

"*Heh.* Oh, yeah. Sorry, pal. Sure it ain't the beer, though?"

Hank shook his empty bottle. "Oh, you're right. I need another!" He shuffled through a cooler. "Drat, we've run dry."

"How's about a *root* beer, then?" Ken suggested.

"Ah, that's right!" Winslow stood, rubbing his hands by the case Ken gifted him. "Let's get us a taste." He freed a bottle. Swirly, vintage lettering decorated the label. "*Ol' Tyme's Root Beer,*" he read, then went for a sip.

"Given the spellin' I thought it was right at your readin' level."

Muirin nudged her son sharply and he wheezed.

"I mean, it's *artisan.* Specially crafted n' all that."

"*Hoo!*" Winslow smacked, drying his beard. "*That's got some spice...*" He coughed. "What's in this? *Gasoline?*"

"Lemme get a sip!" Hank reached.

"It's non-alcoholic, I checked," Ken assured.

Hank sat back. "Never mind."

"Maybe it's one of those drinks they make *taste* alcoholic when it's not?" John suggested.

"All the pain and none of the fun," Becci echoed.

"Who would do such a thing?" Muirin said.

Winslow rubbed his gums. "I thinks me teeth is vibratin'."

Hank grabbed a bottle for himself, relenting, "Ah, what the hey. It's an experience!"

John shrugged. "I'll take one too."

Winslow's eyes watered as he passed out the ghastly concoction, spluttering, "Here y'are. Get 'em while they's deadly."

Becci took one. "I gotta try this." She tinged hers with John's. Even Muirin raised a finger to request one. They drank. Pretty soon, the whole room broke into fits of gags, hacks, and curses.

"*Faith n' begorrah!*" Muirin wailed.

"That'll put hair on your chest," John hissed.

"This tastes radioactive," Becci wheezed.

Ken shook his head blankly amid the upheaval. "I was just tryin' to buy ye some damn candy water—"

Muirin poked him.

"*Gah!* Ain't no kids in 'ere!"

Muirin retracted. "Force o' habit."

All were crying or yelping except Hank, who sucked it down nonchalantly. "Ye all're sissies."

Winslow raised a hand to Ken. "S'alright, Keel. It's a harsh flavor…" He licked his teeth. "But, y'know what? It grows on ya." He chuckled, pointing. "Kinda like you, eh?"

Ken rolled his eyes. "C'mon, now, there's no sauce in that. Quit actin' wild." A smile broke free. "Now, what happened with this… trunky thing?"

"Right!" Winslow wiped his mouth. "Sorry, my lips is numb, hol' on."

Ken sighed.

"Anywho," Winslow resumed, "Trunko was a smart critter t'be sure. He hid out on the Pisces with us till the orcas gave up."

"You sure have a way with these animals," John commented.

"Ya shoulda seen Anna!" Winslow beamed. "The way Trunko was snugglin' up with her, I thought I'd lose me wife ta his charms… li'l rascal." On reflex, Winslow took a swig, then hacked, and continued hoarsely:

"*So*, Anna n' me tried our best ta keep Trunko hid a while longer. I asked her if she was up ta harborin' our furry friend, n' she said, '*Always.*' So, she did her best ta keep 'im from honkin' too much while I ran interference, blockin' the cap'n's view of our stowaway at the stern. Weren't *too* tall a order thankfully; the man's heart was still thuddin' outta his chest from them cranky orcas bashin' his pride n' joy. Weren't sure if he could handle a whole *new species* on his boat too." Winslow swirled the last sip in his bottle. "We *prolly* oughtta clued him in, though. It mighta softened the blow o' what happened next!"

In the glow of the faux fireplace, Winslow's arm rose, and on the faces of his intent listeners he illustrated the rise of a second monster in shadow. His eye quivered. "*This* one was huge. A proper aquatic mammoth! Dabbled in shaggy, white fur, n' trumpetin' loud! If I'da been ashore, I'da thought it the horn of a ship. The sound rippled the water, even, n' the clothes of our cap'n too. N' at all the sensory overload the poor man up n' fainted!"

"Oh, no," Becci giggled.

"Yep. I caught 'im right afore he hit the deck though. Propped 'im up in his chair fer a nap. After that, I walked up ta the big'n. Even got ta pet 'er!"

"What'd it feel like?" John asked.

"*Damp*," Winslow tittered. "She was sheddin' too, unfortunately, so clumps o' her fluff was stickin' t'me. Had a time peelin' it off. Meanwhile, several other trunks went risin' n' trumpetin' in the farther waters. So, Anna guided the youngster back ta the rest o' his herd, n' the family all coasted away t'gether, singin' us a merry melody all the while."

Muirin covered her heart. "So sweet!"

John glinted, lost in vivid imagination of the finned, trunked titans. "I've never heard of anything like that."

"Neither had we. Not till we looked inta it, at least. Turns out they'd done battle with orcas in these waters afore. Some fifty years prior ta our trip, one Trunko lost the fight n' washed up on Margate Beach. Made the papers!"

Becci toasted. "Rightfully so!"

"They thought it *one of a kind*." Winslow's right eye twinkled. "But I can tell ya, there's a whole troupe o' them Trunkos out there, singin' in the sea."

John and Becci beamed. They knew it was true. Muirin was engrossed in the magic herself, hanging on every word. And Ken, though not totally sold, was entertained as ever.

Winslow looked at the picture of him and Anna, misting eyes aglimmer in the fireplace's soft glow. "Whether we was sailin' high with beasts o' legend, or rowin' low with just each other, every day was an adventure in her arms…"

Muirin touched Winslow's elbow. Pensive, Ken looked off, trailing at a thought. He nodded.

Winslow cleared his eyes. "Ah. Where was I?"

"The captain fainted," John said.

"Right. Thanks, Chaplain." Winslow explained, "So, since our cap'n was havin' a snooze, I had ta ferry us back ta shore meself." He chuckled. "I remember glancin' at Anna n' sayin', *'The* one *day we go on vacation, eh?'* "

The room laughed. Winslow eased into the old, worn cushions, the bay thrumming a comforting meter and rocking the houseboat lovingly. His guests were quiet and cozy in the warm glow, content at the pause, and Winslow was just as swept up in the rhythm himself. He concluded:

"We gots back ta harbor no problem. N' when we docked, the cap'n shook awake, ravin' about the crazy dream he just had!"

Ken said, "But it *wasn't* a dream, right?"

Winslow smiled mysteriously. He winked. "Whadda *you* think?"

Ken puffed a laugh from his nose and nodded.

Winslow finished his root beer and smacked. "*Mm.* Y'know, the aftertaste ain't half bad."

After the story, Muirin and Ken said goodbye at the door.

"Thanks fer the tale, lad. Be well," Muirin said.

Winslow leaned to hug her as she pressed a ginger kiss on his cheek. "Sure thing, Mrs. Keel. Thanks."

Ken saluted. "Have a good night, friend."

Winslow shook his hand. "How'd ya like the story?"

"I liked it plenty."

"Ya believe it?"

Ken looked to his mother, then to Winslow, fighting his biases. "There's… always a chance?"

Muirin cooed, "Ye promised not to question a *word* he said, remember?"

Winslow chuckled. "True. Ya did."

Ken shrugged. "I guess it's all real, then."

Winslow pointed. "*Ha!*"

Ken amended, "*Just* for t'night, though!"

"I'll take it. Honestly, I'd be worried fer yer health otherwise." They patted backs. "Still, this's a milestone." As the Keeleys left, Winslow cupped his mouth and called, "I'll be sure ta mention yer conversion down at the eatery next week!"

"*I'll deny it!*"

Winslow smiled. The door clicked shut.

Outside, the night was alive, trilling with nocturnal churrs and croaks, as the Keeleys crossed paths with two other familiar visitors. A tall, pale man with a bristly, white beard, puffy, black jacket, and a sailor's cap walked beside a short woman with a dark complexion and moon-colored eyes, draped in a glittery, purple shawl: Peter and Milly Matterhorn.

Milly's ring-bejeweled fingers clacked as she waved. "Long time no see, dearies!"

Their greetings overlapped and punctuated with hugs, kisses, and handshakes.

"What're ye doin' here?" Ken asked them.

"Checkin' on Wins," Peter explained.

"I heard what happened," Milly added. "So, we brought a cake!"

Peter showed the small, round dessert.

"Couldn't escape the museum till late though. How is he?"

"Oh, better," Ken nodded. "Tellin' tales."

"Which one?"

Muirin jumped in. "One about a sweet li'l ball o' fluff named *Trunko*. He's me new favorite!"

"Ah, I remember that one," Peter said.

Ken smiled. "Ye do?"

Milly stepped closer, whispering, "If you ever have time, stop by the museum. We've got a *fur sample!*"

Ken's face dropped. "Ye do."

"Mm-hm! Exclusive to our collection! And, I'm makin' some cute little plushies o' Trunko too. Might even put on a seminar sometime…"

Ken blinked woozily. "I need to lay down."

When the Matterhorns joined, the party revived for a while. Cake, laughs, and memories were shared even later into the night.

Hank answered his cell phone, standing. "Ahoy Maggie, me sweet." He wandered toward the kitchen. "Aye, I'll be home soon. *Aye*, the beer's gone…"

Becci grinned at the exchange, her eyes flitting to the picture of Winslow and Anna, then to John. He was holding the Cryptolabe.

"What'cha thinking?"

He turned the device over. "Wondering," he finally answered, "how deep it all goes… where this story might take us."

"I'm game if you are."

Milly noticed the tool. "The Cryptolabe!"

Peter groaned, "Don't get her goin' on that thing again."

"Check it out." John popped the lid.

Milly hopped up. "You got it to open?!"

"What've you done?" Peter moaned.

John showed her. "The emblem's a button."

"I *tried* that, it didn't work. *Peter* tried that." She spun to him, beads and jewels clattering. "You didn't press hard enough!"

"Thing's old, Mill!"

"*You're* old!"

At the commotion, Winslow returned to the room, eye bulging at the item in John's hands.

"Where'd ya get that?"

Milly waved from the couch. "Finally passed the puzzle on to the next generation."

Winslow swallowed. "Oh."

"We're thinking of writing a story on it," John revealed. "On the agents."

"I wouldn't."

"They've been seen around town still," Becci added.

Winslow's throat bobbed. "That so."

"People are a little weirded out about it. We're trying to figure out what's going on."

"What does it do?" John asked.

"Nothin'. Don't worry about it."

John relented, arm dropping. He didn't want to press any further; the topic seemed to make Winslow uncomfortable. But, as the purple needle in the

Cryptolabe's glass dome rattled, and his mind flashed with the scene from the obscure toy commercial, he felt himself ask, "What are K-fields?"

Winslow's eye quivered. His lips repeated the term as his brow stitched, then he hobbled into the kitchen without saying a word.

John straightened up, worried. He hoped he hadn't deflated the night, especially after how great everyone's spirits were. Hank munched on the last piece of cake and uttered a stuffed groan, before watching Winslow pull open the sliding glass door and step onto the now-rainy balcony to stare down the dark waves, pull out the bosun pipe, and whistle.

John slumped back in the couch. *Why did I say that?* he wondered. He traded concerned looks with Becci. *I should've left it alone.*

Winslow came back, different. When he plopped into his chipping, red chair by the fake fire, Hank, Milly, Peter, John, and Becci all leaned in. He didn't seem torn up like the night before; there was a blend of emotions in his eyes. Some relief, some panic, John interpreted, before he reconsidered it as a look of wild, sudden clarity.

"Hank," Winslow spoke. "I know what I gotta do."

"Aye, Wins? What's the thing?"

"Two things," Winslow clarified. He smoothed his beard, as his stare landed on his collection of mementos from his past. "One only I can do." His eye flicked to the Cryptolabe next. "The other'll require a fair bit o' smarts n' wit."

Becci gestured to John and herself. "That's our middle names!" She patted John. "You're *Wit*."

Winslow's mind raced. "It's dangerous."

"Yeah, what else is new?"

"We'll help however we can," John promised, projecting all his certainty through his eyes.

Winslow squinted. His jaw shifted.

"Anythin' ye need," Hank added.

"Anythin'," Peter echoed.

"We're here for you." Milly said.

Winslow lifted his chin. "Got yer recorder?" As John patted down his coat pockets to find it, Winslow said to Hank, "It *is* all connected." He nodded. "Ya were right."

"Well," Hank shrugged, "I *am* a genius."

"Got it." John held up the device, firelight flickering on its sleek, black case.

"I ain't told many folks 'bout these parts o' me past. Most wouldn't believe it. But I gots ta make things right." He took a shaky breath. "N' I need help." In the glow, Winslow's buggy eye fixed on John and his readied recorder. "Ya sure ya wanna hear, Chaplain?" His features were serious as ever. "This one's gonna blow yer mind."

John swallowed. He held the recorder, then glanced at Becci. She nodded.

The button clicked.

The Way I Sees It

*idn't want nothin' ta do with it at the time… Didn't think it concerned me. I remember some o' the suits' scientists yammerin' about 'fluxes' n'… bio… magneto… somethin' er other — I dunno…"*

The recorded voice of Winslow Hoffner crackled through a cylindrical speaker jostling in Becci's purse, propped up in the center of the truck's bench seat, as the old vehicle rumbled down the swerving, waterside road.

"The theory really started gainin' traction when our sister organization observed some 'unusual qualities' with this critter they scooped up on the shores o' Canvey Island. They didn't get ta complete their research though, 'cause — " He snorted. *"Well, that's a story fer another time…"*

A Nova Scotia license plate tapped loosely below the truck's rusted grille as its gruff engine tittered.

When asked to expand on K-fields, Winslow went on, *"Whether the critters actually made the energy or responded ta it, they didn't know. They figured it musta been a bit o' both. They even made machines ta try n' 'read the fields.' "*

"The Cryptolabe…"

"Aye, Chaplain. That was the first one, anyhow. Weren't as reliable as they'd hoped, but it worked enough ta get 'em workin' on the next one… one that could 'bend the fields,' whatever than means. 'Course that one didn't work at all!" Winslow laughed. *"Not the way they wanted it to at least. All it really did was put the rest o' their equipment on the fritz… Point is, none of 'em were* exactly *sure what this energy was afore they started foolin' with it. Tryin' ta control it. N' if that ain't the biggest crime, I dunno what is. Classic suits though."*

"At least they's consistent, eh?" Hank Malloy commented in the background of the recording.

"Aye. N' on account o' that, I gots a good feelin' o' where you two can find s'more material fer yer story — maybe more'n ya bargained fer — not ta mention a way ta keep our legendary pals in the bay free from… whatever the suits is doin'. But, from what I can recall, yer gonna needs a truck ta haul this thingamajig back. Hope ya can drive a stick, Chaplain…"

In the driver's seat of Winslow's red pickup, John Chaplain's fingers clutched firm to the wheel. He felt his chest muscles tighten as his mind strained to sort out all the information Winslow had revealed to them: the mysterious corners of the world he traversed in his youth where honest debates were had—not on the existence of those legendary beasts John came to know as *cryptids*—but instead on the classifications of those cryptids, and how to track them.

In the passenger seat, Becci Hamrin turned to notice John's disquieted features. She paused the interview's playback, clicked her pen and flipped her notepad shut. "You alright?"

John wrung the wheel. "I'm fine. It's... just a lot, you know?"

"Yeah." Becci nodded. "Another day, another earth-shattering revelation."

They chuckled. In the silence that followed, John reflected on how drastically his life, and his understanding of the world, had changed in such a short period of time. And when he pressed that button on his recorder the other night, he was plunged even deeper into the world as Winslow Hoffner saw it.

There were hidden places, the reporters learned. Locked-away places at the absolute edge of human understanding—where science and magic were discussed with interchangeable feasibility—and now, John and Becci were on a road trip to one of them.

The whole night prior, John had found himself pacing through his apartment, trying to sort out everything he had learned, all while checking his email for the go-ahead from Albert to take this investigative trip with Becci. Occasionally he'd play parts of the interview, dart to his keyboard to rough out a structure for the story, then inevitably backspace, leaving the cursor blinking in wait.

Mentally he was still there, it felt like. Only the pattering of rain and his restless, pacing shadow cast by the glow of his monitor accompanied him, until a text from Becci vibed on his phone.

As if psychically linked, she wrote, *You still up too?*

Yep, he replied.

Cool, I thought I was the only weirdo haha.

John smiled. *You're good. Either that or we're both going insane at the same time.*

Distinct possibility.

John relayed his difficulty outlining the piece, and Becci contended the story would emerge naturally as they went. John's sight rested on the Cryptolabe on his desk, brass lid highlighted by the blue glow of his computer. Now, that same relic jangled from its chain, hanging under the rearview mirror of Winslow's loaned pickup, and John's lingering worries from yesternight were quelled by Becci's upbeat conviction:

"It'll all work out in the end." She reclined a little in the stiff passenger seat. "And hey, it's better than whatever assignment Nell would've given us."

"True," John nodded. "He was weirdly onboard with this one, though." John remembered the email that ultimately came through late last night, not from Albert but from the assistant editor, which approved the requested trip with a single line:

Take all the time you need, Johnny.

Nell's support was more disturbing than his subversions ever were.

John reasoned, "Maybe he just wanted to get rid of us for a while."

"Works for me." Becci opened a bag of chips. "The feeling's mutual. I could do with a little less drama for a few days."

"You sure this is the story for that?"

Becci crunched and shrugged. "Well, I mean, less *Nell* drama. I'll take monsters and magic over bleachy any day."

The two laughed, and John eased, consistently amazed by Becci's attitude in the face of the unknown. "Yeah," he agreed. "At least we're in charge of our own destiny this way."

Becci's eyes flashed. "Oh!" She licked the salt from her fingertips. "Speaking of *destiny*, did I tell you about my interview with Mrs. McCottry?"

"The woman who filed the police report about the agents? No, how did that go?"

"It went great, until we recognized each other."

"What do you mean?"

Becci smiled awkwardly and expounded, "Remember that old woman that was shushing me at Keeley's… the one I, uh, kinda snapped at?"

When John made the connection, his eyebrows shot up. "You're kidding."

"Same woman."

"Oh, *geez!*" John laughed. "What happened?"

"Well, she chased me around her garden, lecturing me about respect, threatening to retract all her statements... When I tried to apologize, she thought I was shushing her *again* —"

"Oh, no."

"Yeah. That's when she *really* exploded... and the neighbors came out—" Becci sighed and waved her hand at the air. "It was a whole thing." She checked left and beamed, matching John's brightened expression. "The joys of journalism, right? Anyway, long story short, I pulled a Milly and brought her a cake early this morning to smooth things over."

John swiped a post-laughter tear from his eye. "Did that work?"

Becci munched on a chip. "Yeah, we're cool now, believe it or not. She said she likes my 'moxie.' "

John blinked, impressed. "Huh. Just like that?"

"Yep."

"That must've been some cake."

"*And* she wants to set me up with her nephew."

John's face stretched in awe. He joked, "Did you put anything extra in the icing? Is 'moxie' not what I think it is?"

Becci winked and put a finger over her lips. "*Ssshh...*"

Spirits enlivened, Becci flipped her notepad open and pressed the play button on the recorder. Winslow's voice crackled back over the speaker: "*Ain't too sure if the answer ta this riddle lies in the present or the past. Maybe it's a bit o' both. The way I sees it, there are two roads...*"

The red pickup squeaked, blundering by a sign that read, *Now Leaving Bayfield.*

"*As fer me, there's somethin' I gotta do. Somethin' I've had ta do fer a while now, actually, but I'm only just realizin' it.*" A breath of pause fuzzed through. "*Some memories take a li'l longer ta decode, I s'pose...*"

"Ye sure ye don' want comp'ny?" Hank asked, his teal sedan puttering to a stop outside the airport. "I know those parts well, ye know."

"I'm sure. This's somethin' I gotta do on me own." Winslow nodded. "Y'know, I kept a lot o' mementos from me travels, but this'n..." He blinked, then shook his head. "I gots a hard time lettin' go."

"It'll be alright."

"I know. I mean, I hope so. I just... wonder if things'll be back ta normal after all this."

"Normal?"

"Aye."

Hank thought a moment, then told him, "Maybe. But, I have tae tell ye friend, you're the oddest man I know. I dinnae think ye were ever meant for a normal life."

"That's," Winslow chuckled, "comfortin'."

"Ye were meant for somethin' *grander*. Bolder, louder!" Hank pumped his fist triumphantly. "Considerin' the adventures ye have on accident... Lord, I can only *imagine* what great n' wondrous magic ye'll loose on the world, should ye heed a beckonin' o' the soul."

Winslow smiled and unclicked his seatbelt. "Thanks, Hank."

Hank patted his friend's shoulder before he exited the car. "Don' mention it." Then, his brow danced at an idea, and he leaned to call out the open window, "Ye know what? I think I'm gonna get some shoppin' done while you're away."

Winslow slung his bag over his shoulder. "Yeah? Fer what?"

"*Haw*, it's a surprise!" Hank shifted into drive and peeled out, while Winslow chuckled a little, shifted his weight, hooked his thumb on the strap of his luggage, and tried to hold his first mate's words in his mind as he strode into the airport terminal.

Plopping into a seat, he turned at the whimpering sounds of a passenger's pet, nervous claws tapping on metal. The shine of small, black eyes in a cage beside him captured his focus.

"*May not seem like it, but it'll be alright,*" he whispered to the terrier.

The bustle of voices around him blended, blurred, and rhymed with the nighttime murmurs of a far-off, Conwy tavern. He breathed, air tinged with scents from the past.

"*It'll be alright,*" he spoke, mostly to himself, as the memories flooded over him.

A plate of steamy mollusks sizzled in front of Tobias Kabel in the corner of an old, Conwy tavern called the *Trinity Inn.*

"Danke," the giant thanked their server, before slurping down the meal voraciously, shells clacking in a messy, wet stack. He offered some to his deckhand friend, whose stomach lurched at the sight of them.

"Ain't hungry fer anythin' in a shell," the young man admitted.

"Mm." Kabel waved. "*Wunderschöne,*" he flagged their waitress and winked. "Bring my friend somesing zat isn't in a shell, ja? Maybe somesing sveet." He checked Winslow's reaction, then amended, "To go."

Winslow shook his head. "Don't understand how ya can even eat at this hour, Kabel."

Kabel flexed. "A machine zis great requires plenty of *fuel,* Kamerad." He held up a wiggly glob. "Und zat fuel is *protein!*" He munched down the last clam.

"Why're we here, anyway?"

Kabel licked his fingers. "I'm vaiting."

"Fer what?"

"For you to tell me zee truth."

Winslow frowned. "I thought ya believed me 'bout the Morgawr… ya said ya knew about it—"

Kabel laughed. "I do. It's not zat."

"What then? The mermaid? Ya can ask Richter, he saw it too."

"Richter can't remember vat he had for breakfast," Kabel chuckled. "Zat's not it either, though." He patted his abs and set his plate aside to be bussed. "I believe *all* your stories, Winslow. It's not vat you've told me." His brow lifted. "It's vat you *haven't*."

Winslow started shakily, "I…"

Kabel smiled. "Zis isn't an interrogation, Kamerad. I've seen you're different. Somesing happened, ja?"

"S'fine. Don't worry 'bout it."

"Vell, I'm here if you vant to get anysing off your chest. No pressure."

"Bloody Liar?"

"*Huh?*" Both men turned at the same time.

Their waitress held up a dessert item, wrapped in foil. "Bloody Liar," the curly-haired woman repeated. "Our house dessert. It's like a doughnut but extra large, extra crispy, and chock full o' jam!"

"Why's it called the Bloody Liar?" Winslow asked.

" 'Cause you'll always eat more than you should," the waitress leaned in with a wink and a whisper, *"but you'll never admit it!"*

Winslow smiled and nodded.

The waitress bounced in place, adding, "It's the chef's mam-gu's recipe actually. There's a funny story about—"

"Danke." Kabel snatched the wrapped-up dessert, chuckling, "My friend could stand to put on a few." He leaned across the table and tucked it in the inner pocket of Winslow's oversized, gray dress jacket, then patted his chest. "Get any skinnier und you'll slip through zee floorboards!" Kabel watched the woman disappear, then looked back to Winslow. "Anyvay..." He checked that they were alone again, then said, "Things have been odd lately, haven't zey?"

Winslow's gaze strayed, tracking the rocky seams in the repurposed castle walls to the Celtic designs in a stained glass window that looked to have been salvaged from an old chapel. Diffused, golden light, fractured by metal armature, cast broken, angled shapes on the seafarer's uncertain features. His pensive stare eventually settled on the flickering flame of a brass candle sconce.

"Monsters…" Kabel's electric eyes shone brightly in the cavernous space. "Zey're real."

"Yeah, yer tellin' me," Winslow shivered.

"You haven't been yourself since our last drop." Kabel picked his teeth. "Ven zee cargo got avay." He squinted, tracking the deckhand's fidgets. "Vat *really* happened?"

Winslow stared back at him for a long time, reading his eyes.

"You can trust me," Kabel assured. "I vant to help you."

Winslow's mind reeled. This world was new to him, and Kabel seemed calmer and more receptive to these discussions than most. Kabel had been steeped in legends longer than he, as it turned out, and for a moment Winslow felt a pulse of genuineness in his crewmate's concerns. The young sailor checked over his shoulder, then leaned in. "Alright."

"*Alright.*" Kabel rubbed his huge hands.

Winslow gripped the edge of the table. "The small crate at the last drop… it busted open, right?"

"I remember."

"And I chased the critter inta the brush fer a time."

"Ja."

"But I fell n' rolled some, till the forest spat me out at the base o' this glittery lake. I heard a snap, n' a shriek. I went after the sound…"

Kabel frowned. "Ja?"

"N' I saw it. I saw the seal," Winslow said. "It was barkin', hurt, with its back flipper chomped in a trap." He swallowed. "I heard ya'll hollerin' somethin' behind me but I couldn't tell where ya were; it was like… the forest was swallowin' up the sound."

"So zee seal *didn't* get avay —"

"Naw. I freed it."

Kabel's nostrils flared. "Winslow…"

"I wedged a stick in the trap n' pried it open."

"Do you know how *expensive* zat seal —?"

"It don't matter, Kabel. And it *weren't* a seal."

Kabel frowned.

"At least, it didn't stay that way." Winslow's lip twitched. He rocked forward. "I don't think ya know what it is we're tradin'. I think if ya did, ya wouldn't wanna do it no more."

Kabel breathed. "Tell me."

"After I freed her, she..." Winslow's eye twitched. "It was unbelievable..."

"Vat?"

"When the seal was free, her fur dropped—or kinda peeled back, like a bag. N' outta the empty pelt, this glowin' light stepped out."

"*Stepped?*"

"Yeah, like a person," Winslow jittered. "But made o' *white light*. Her hair was flowin' all 'round like she was underwater too. She came toward me. I-I couldn't bring m'self ta move... I dunno what it was." Winslow's eyes fluttered.

Kabel's got wide. "A Selkie."

"A what?"

"A water spirit—a shape-shifter. I've heard stories of zem, but I never..." Kabel shook his head. "Go on, Kamerad. Vat'd she do?"

Seeing he was believed, Winslow enlivened. "Well, as she passed by the trees, her glow was... Aw, I don't even know how ta say it—"

"*Try.*"

Winslow's eyes shimmered, almost reflecting the memory of his encounter with the water spirit. "The hair on me arm stood on end; the grass seemed ta do the same, while dewdrops from the blades rose n' suspended in midair—li'l spheres o' water reflectin' spectrums o' color. Color like I'd never seen afore... Then, the animals joined in, like her presence was rattlin' alert all the critters o' the forest—they was singin'!"

"Singing?"

"Yeah. In *sounds* like I'd never heard afore. The trees was choirin' in harmony too: catchin' the sea breezes in slopey boughs, melodizin' 'em in leafy lungs..."

Kabel frowned, but stayed engaged.

"Then, she made this symbol." Winslow tried to emulate the Selkie's three-fingered gesture: index finger high and thumb angled out, across from his middle. "Like this. N' she pushed her hand inta me chest." He pressed the shape forward. "Like *this.*"

Winslow fell back in his creaky chair. "She hardly touched me, but I was blown back. Felt like lightning struck." Winslow's eyes flashed. "Yeah, I think lightning *did* strike, actually. I remember now. A big bolt came down on the lake, boilin' it some, n' settin' all them floatin' dewdrops a'sparkle..." Winslow checked his listener's still face, as his own twitched with worry. "I'm tellin' ya the *truth*, Kabel."

"I know, I know. It's alright." He reached across the table and cupped the young man's shoulder. "I believe you."

"Ya do?"

"Ja. I can tell." He smiled. "You're a terrible liar, remember?"

Winslow returned a grin. "Aye, ya said that." He shook his head. "All these things that've happened. They felt like dreams..." A chill hit him. "But they ain't dreams, are they?" Wind was howling through an open window now. Its rippling, black curtains matched the tattered rags that draped the first crate Winslow had ever traded. "They're real." Winslow's mind burned and his focus blurred as he twisted at the recollection in shame. He clawed the table. "That's why we gotta stop this."

Kabel frowned. "Stop vat?"

Winslow clamored, "Weren't ya *listenin'*? What we're foolin' with — what we're tradin'. It's magic. It's legendary." The deckhand gulped. "It's pure."

Kabel nodded.

"I can't be part o' whatever's happenin' here," Winslow went on. "N' I don't think *you* oughtta be either. Yer a good man, Kabel. Ya don't wanna be another cog in a machine. Ya wanna do yer own thing — ya've said that."

"Ja..." His friend picked up his glass and set it down a couple of times. "I alvays said, 'one more, one more... zen I'm out...' "

"Right. We can end it here."

"You're right." The heavy mug clunked one more time, as Kabel's electric eyes struck his friend. "I sink vee can."

The glass mug rang. So did Winslow's ears. The deckhand frowned, as the image of the tavern blurred, blotting with dark, pulsing with screams, then hazing with waves of pain and numbness. The time between their friendly discussion at the tavern and what happened next was beaten out of his memory.

"Make 'im talk!"

"Where's the Selkie?"

His attackers' roars were muffled by the ringing, as the deckhand was thrown around a malicious circle in a dungeonous, underground chamber, lit with torches and echoing with a hostility more medieval than its walls.

The young man grunted, throwing a punch that went nowhere, then catching a fist in his jaw. He twisted and slammed onto the rocky floor, lines of foamy, crimson spit swinging from his lower lip. The pause was long enough for aches to throb back to the surface of his skin. He gurgled a yell as he was dragged back up to his knees.

"Where's the Selkie?" a backlit brute grated.

Winslow rolled free and jumped with a staggering punch to his questioner's nose, who shrieked and fell away while two others viced his arms.

Winslow squirmed. To his right, he saw blood-dotted money trading fists over a crude fighting ring. Inside, what looked like a striped, dog-sized, emaciated otter was forced into battle with an equally-starved, shelled, mammalian creature swinging a spiky club-tail. Mysterious things, plucked from prehistory and the pages of mythology, made to bite and claw at each other for dark entertainment.

To his left were dapper villains doing business like nothing was amiss, leafing through booklets and marking tallies beside colorful illustrations of handsome and strange creatures: tall, flightless birds, multiheaded snakes, winged amphibians. Some even dined; thick, metallic steam wafted from a lifted cloche, where silver plates bore roasted animals, the skulls of which possessed horns and sockets like nothing the natural world had yet documented.

All around were stacks of dingy, filth-coated crates of varying sizes that rattled with traumatized shrieks. None of the gamblers, bidders, or scoundrels seemed too fazed by them. Some even agitated otherwise-silent captives with electric shock-sticks prodded through their crates' barred doors, then chortled at the shadowy convulsions therein.

And ahead, standing just above and beyond the piles of pain and brutality, emerged the sorry face of Tobias Kabel.

"Just tell zem where zee Selkie is, Kamerad."

Winslow spat, mumbling. When Kabel stepped forward to ask what was uttered, Winslow gritted, "I said I ain't yer Kamerad."

The giant's blue eyes sparkled and nose cringed as his friend took a heavy kick to the stomach. "Be reasonable!"

The thug with the broken nose slogged up again and grappled Winslow's collar, spitting red. "*Where. Is. The Selkie?*"

Winslow's woozy head lifted to his bystanding crewmate. "That's a question."

Kabel's chest deflated, as more fists fell. He whispered something to one of the other dark watchers, who paused, then nodded, before Kabel clopped up the stone steps and into a flickering, candlelit hallway.

Winslow spat, squeezing out a hoarse call to his betrayer: "Best way ta *get* along is ta *go* along, huh, Kabel?"

Kabel returned a morose look.

Winslow took another punch, then another, the last one connecting with a crack that made even the attackers pause and reel. *"Ooh!"*

Red bubbles fizzed through Winslow's teeth. He spat one out, staining his scraggled, blond beard, then gasped a pained whistle. *"I'm* gettin' along *great."* He broke into aching, sardonic chuckles as he was beaten down, and Kabel disappeared. *"I'm..."* he woozed, *"gettin' along..."*

"Ee's a tough sonuvabitch ain't ee?"

"Take 'im to Shaull. Ee'll fix 'im."

Clocked sideways, dragged hard against the gritty floor, then propped up before the lip of a circular pit at the center of the chamber, Winslow coughed, as the fiend Kabel had whispered to stepped through the torchglow and knelt, shadowed save for the shine of his circular lenses.

"Your friend wants us to keep you alive."

"Oo gives a rat's wot 'is friend wonts?!" the thug with the shattered nose spluttered.

The shadow they called Shaull covered the maniac's fist. "Easy, Stokes. We're *reasonable* men." A disturbing smile shined through the shade of the man's hat. "We won't kill you." As his head tipped, bands of firelight flickered over a triad of clawmarks dragging over his mouth and chin. "As for the *monsters* you're so passionate for…"

A black boot knocked what little air was left from Winslow's chest, and he tumbled backward into the pit, slamming hard into the thin layer of hay over the sharp rock floor.

"*That* is another story."

Stokes wiped the blood from his upper lip, snickering as he watched horror flash on the young deckhand's face, then commented, "You's a master of compromise, Shaull."

Winslow pushed himself up achingly. Throngs of evil gathered to chant above him, as his vision tunneled on a large, familiar crate at the far end of the pit. It had been repurposed: sides mortared and bolted to the stone wall as a square tunnel to a dark, cave-like antechamber, but identical in every other way. Ripped, black cloth covered the bars on its front. Shadows and howls rolled within, as a puff of hot rage blew forward the rags and rippled the frayed edges of Winslow's gray dress jacket.

Winslow panted and paled. He staggered, clawing to climb the sides of the pit, only to be kicked back down or prodded at by sparking, metal prongs. He grunted, heart thudding, and his wild eyes fixed on the cage-like doors that contained the mystery. Fiery eyeshine glinted back—the eyes of the first beast he traded so many months ago.

Rusted, crisscrossed, iron chains rumbled, cranked on either side of the hollow by gangsters above, while Shaull hissed:

"Release the Afanc."

The Critter in the Crate

eavy impacts pounded, racing up the bruised legs and vibrating in the sore solar plexus of the stranded seafarer, as small fibers of hay on the stone floor jounced, hovered, settled, then shot up again with the next quaking footfall of the beast, stomping free from shadow.

The man called Shaull raised his arms to the crowd, and through a scarred smile heralded their champion monster, "*Behold!* The demon of Wales!"

Cheers echoed as teeth entered first: overlapped fangs sprouting from leathery, crocodilian-shaped jaws. They clapped at the riotous shadows above as its brown eyes dilated in the torchglow. The Afanc was the size of a bear, with overgrown, hooked claws to match, curving from webbed paws on its trunky legs. A flat tail dragged behind, flapping, leathery appearance akin to that on its snout. It thumped at the center of the pit, fully lit. Blood-matted, dark brown fur swung loosely on a sunken stomach. Its dagger-like teeth unlaced with webs of famished spit, and its hoarse throat bellowed a deep, rolling roar—like that of a grizzly blended with something primordial—priming the appetite of its watchers for violence.

"*Per-ci-val! Per-ci-val!*" the chamber chanted the Afanc's name as it charged, heavy gallop matching rhythm and echoing into drum-like beats. Winslow scrambled backward.

"Easy there, Percy—*Hey!*" He jumped aside as the monster barreled, slamming snout-first into the wall, leaving cracks in the stone. It clacked an agitated growl and shook, as the crowd above booed and chucked things. It roared.

"I ain't with them," Winslow panted. A crushed beer can clunked off the Afanc's head. Its pupils shrank into angry dots. "I just got here—!"

The cylindrical crater pounded with a whorl of menacing, monstrous howls, some from the beast, some from the cretins above, as sharp serrations of teeth clapped for Winslow's face. The sailor put his hands up, catching the top jaw with his right and the lower with his left. His worn, brown shoes scraped back and the crowd exploded in excited shrills, as he was pressed toward the wall.

There, Winslow's heels clattered through a pile of bones. He gulped, hoping they weren't human, then buckled low.

Above, he heard the whispers of the criminals echo and magnify off the rock walls:

"Don't make sense."

"That's what ee said. No lake. Sumfin don't add up."

One, closer, appealed, *"Shaull, I 'eard word from Voss. Ee wonts to talk to 'im."*

"Voss isn't here," Shaull hissed back.

The Afanc pushed its gladiator into the skeletal pile, biting. The crowd cheered, but when the combatants resurfaced, Winslow was unscathed, and a large bone was wedged vertically between the Afanc's jaws. Outrage boomed, as cans and pebbles rained down, this time on Winslow.

"I'm in the same boat, y'see?" he wheezed.

Percival's nostrils puffed and jaws muscled down, snapping the femur.

"Alright, have it yer way." Winslow grabbed another bone to defend himself, batting away the animal's lunges.

"Voss says ee'll cut us in double *if we keep 'im breathing. Says it's the biggest score we'll ever see."*

Shaull grated back, *"And if he tells us now, it'll be our score."* He shouted, "Feel like talking yet?!"

Winslow's mind raced. *"Hey,"* he whispered to the beast.

It snapped and he batted.

"Hey!"

It warbled a clacking growl.

"I'm sorry, alright?" Winslow opened the arms of his oversized, scratchy dress jacket. "Fer… everythin'. I didn't know." As the emaciated monster skulked, Winslow dropped the bone, showed his palms, and continued, "I still don't know much, but, maybe you n' me can work t'geth—"

CLUNK! A projectile lobbed from above bashed Winslow in the side of the head, knocking him out.

The Afanc sniffed the collapsed man's chest.

"Idiots!" Shaull roared to the spectators. "Get him out of there!"

Before they had the chance, the monster scooped up the sailor in its mouth, growling and flapping its tail at any who reached too close.

"No… no!" Shaull yelled, as one of the Afanc's sharp teeth punctured the jacket, and a dark red stream gushed. It carried Winslow's limp body back into its lair, growling in the shadows.

No stranger to pain, the incoming attacks on the seafarer's face lost their initial shock. Only the echo of hurt could pulse through now, humming under the numbness between a blur of fists and a roar of demanding screams, until a new, calmer intonation disbanded the chaos for a sore moment.

The young sailor lifted a wounded, icy glare to his assailants: a bruised-and-battered Shaull and a terrified, twitching Stokes, both of whom backed into the shadows as their spectral superior slunk into the light and took a seat across the metal table. He smiled broadly. Winslow frowned.

The looming newcomer was buttoned in a dark, weathered, leather jacket. Where visible on the inside of the cuffs and collar, a lining of bright crimson burned. His hat was banded by some kind of snakeskin that was strung and coroneted with a variety of pointed fangs. And on his shoulders, a spotty, white pelt caped him. Winslow squinted, unsure to what animal it once belonged. But the shadowy wearer's hand intermittently rose to pet it, as though soothing the corpse.

"Good evening, Mr. Hoffner," he greeted. Winslow could detect a subtle, Germanic influence to his pronunciations—though not as overt as those of the Trident's crew—and with a cadence that evidenced the blended, chameleonic accent of a far-traveled man. "Your friend Kabel tells me of your exploits."

"Friend..."

"Or, should I say, the *stories* of your exploits. A mermaid in the North Sea, a Morgawr here in the harbor... among others..." He petted the pelt on his shoulder. "I must say, you have made quite the impression in such a short time."

Winslow cringed, wiggling into as comfortable a sit as his restrained arms allowed, and sucking blood through his teeth. "Ya sure know a lot about me n' I know nothin' about you."

"How cruel of me." The man's voice was hollow, rickety, cold, and precise—creeping upon him like a chill through a catacomb—and yet, it was darkly blithe, as though constantly restraining the urge to burst into hyenic hysterics. The shade introduced himself, savoring every syllable:

"My name is Bin Burkhart Voss."

"That yer whole name?"

"You may call me *Binnie* if you prefer."

Winslow seethed. "Naw. I don't think I will."

"Too cuddly?" Voss leaned into the heavy light, shadowing angled shapes on his pallid face and the demented, sunken hollows that framed his pyrite-colored eyes. "Have you learned what we do here?"

"I take it it ain't a pettin' zoo."

"Intuitive." Voss chuckled. "For some people, *exotic* isn't exotic enough. We simply provide the very particular demand of a very particular clientele." Voss' smile stretched. He was somehow scowling and smirking at the same time. "It is so good to finally meet you, Mr. Hoffner," he continued. "I have a feeling you and I are going to be *great* friends."

"That so."

"Yes. Like you, I am quite *intuitive*." He stroked the fur on his shoulder. "Now that introductions are out of the way…" His upper lip curled, stare flicking at the empty crates scattered around the blank room. "Perhaps you can share with me where you've taken my treasures?"

"Nowhere—"

"I can only imagine…" Voss spoke over his captive, musing, pensive. "What a *feat* to have charmed so many fearsome beasts—without so much as a *scratch*—"

"Well, Shaull took the lion's share o' the scratches," Winslow taunted, rising. "Ain't that right, Shaull?"

Shadows rippled as Shaull limped in, fist balled. Voss waved him back.

"Ah-ah. Don't be so thin-skinned, my friend." Shaull recoiled. Voss got comfortable. "Forget their whereabouts." He grinned. "I'm just curious. *How* did you do it? I'm sure it was quite a *thrilling* endeavor."

Winslow tried to decode the madman's odd expressions but came up short. "Whadda *you* care?"

"I want to know what all the fuss is about."

"What *fuss?*"

"Do what you do best." Voss leaned forward. "Tell me a story."

Winslow squinted, then puffed a breath through his nose.

"Ee's killed 'im!"

"Voss is gonna kill us!"

"Shuttup, you fools!"

"It's over!"

"It's not *over. Get down there!"*

With a wheezing, whistling cough, Winslow gasped awake in the Afanc's lair, shooting up. At a cold wetness he patted his chest, feeling a sticky, red residuum on his shirt, but finding no injury beneath it. He frowned, then looked across the antechamber at the Afanc, who had snatched the sailor's dress jacket and was nibbling at something inside.

Percival clawed away a foil wrapper as his jaws snuffled to free the "Bloody Liar" doughnut from the inside pocket of the rags, an obscene gush of messy, berry jam cascading over his fangs and chin fur.

"Nice one," Winslow murmured. "Even fooled me." He limped over, grabbing the stained, tattered remnants of his jacket. Both sleeves were ripped off.

The Afanc hooted.

"Nah, it's cool. I, uh… like it better this way." Winslow dragged it on. "See? It's a vest," he laughed achingly, then coughed, "Thanks."

Getting a closer, calmer look at the face of the animal, the patterns on the snout that once resembled reptilian scales now seemed more like the cracking abrasions of a scarred, dehydrated bill. While the Afanc was certainly capable of doing damage with those jaws and the elaborate fangs that armed them, the way they clacked and shook on the meal made Winslow reconsider the legend's origins. With that, his fear subsided, watching the hulking mammal clap down the sticky morsels of the doughnut, snarfing and lapping with dog-like jollity on his treat.

"You enjoy that, Percy."

Winslow noticed more bones cluttering the cave of the Afanc. The mangled work of a ham-handed butcher, it looked like. What scraps of torn meat remained on those femurs and ribcages seemed to have been picked at out of desperation rather than predatory crave.

"Ya deserve it," Winslow added, sliding down the wall into a grunting half-sit, before rising again at the sound of gangsters approaching. The sailor swallowed and backed into the shadows.

The brutish one called Stokes stepped in, metal keys clattering on his belt. He peeked, seeing the Afanc feasting messily and shuddered, "Ee's eatin' 'im, Shaull..."

"Get back, you imbecile," Shaull scolded. He treaded in himself, a two-pronged, metal shock-stick sparking in his hand. His scarred face curled in disgust, uttering, "*Filthy beast...*" then poising his weapon.

Percival roared.

Before Shaull could strike, a hefty, meaty bone clonked on the back of his head, knocking off his glasses and dropping the shocker from his grip. From outside, he seemed to trip, grunting, then gasting at the swing of the monster's massive tail. "*Wha — ?!*"

THOOMPH! Shaull's body rocketed sideways into the cave wall and flumped over a clatter of bones. The brutes outside screamed for their stolen comrade. Stokes raced in, but caught the backswing of Percival's paddle himself and hurtled backward into the pit, where he and the others could only watch, as the Afanc prowled into the shadowed part of its cave, maw gaping with gore-colored stains.

Winslow peeked around the corner at the hollering men, then grabbed a handful of smaller bones from the pile.

"Shaull? *Shaull?!*" someone called outside.

As Percival made a low, rolling growl, Winslow heaved the bones from the shadows. They scattered over the pit and knocked near the henchmen's feet. They screamed.

"Oh God, ee got 'im! Percival got Shaull!"

"Peeled 'is flesh off 'is bones in two seconds!"

"How'd he do that?!"

"I don't wanna find out. Run! *Run!*"

They scrambled over one another, shrieking to escape the pit.

The audience of criminals above panicked and abandoned their entertainers, forcing them to claw up the sides of the pit themselves, while others frantically ran to the cranks to drop the bars and seal the horror in its cave. Chains rumbled, and Winslow scurried to punt a ribcage between the doors, catching in the space between to leave a gap.

Winslow's chest pounded, body jittery with adrenaline as he panted and listened to the fading wails of the criminals above pouring out of the chamber in a stampede, fear of the monster eclipsed only by the mentions of a suspected furious reprisal by Voss.

Winslow waited longer for the screams to dissipate into eerie, abandoned silence, before striding alongside his beastly cellmate, who sniffed the unceremoniously-splayed body of Shaull. Winslow found the crook's glasses on the floor and held one lens under his nose. It fogged with breath.

"Nighty night," the sailor mumbled. He looted the gangster's shock-stick and wangled it through his belt loop, hooking it like a sword. "Might be handy."

Percival clacked his bill, as Winslow crept through the crate-tunnel and inspected the slim space he'd managed to save between the metal doors, wedged open by bone. It was just enough for a rail-thin man like himself to squeeze through. And on the floor of the pit, left behind in the hectic scramble, a ring of keys laid waiting.

Winslow's grin sparkled. "What's say you n' me get outta here, Percy?"

When he squeezed through, Percival clacked and warbled, pressing his bill against the bars. "I ain't leavin' ya. I promise."

The Afanc chattered.

Winslow made it to the other side. He pocketed the key ring, then spotted the slack of the chains dangling above. He leapt, swung, and tugged. The space between the double doors widened a few inches. Percival shoved his bill through, grunting.

"Take it easy. Almost there," Winslow told him. He dug his heels in on the wall and yanked, until one of the barred doors dragged open enough for Percival to muscle a shoulder through and thrash, bashing the other off its track. It hit the far wall of the pit, and the chain in Winslow's hand loosed.

"*Whoa!*" the sailor whooped as he fell, but landed safely on a leathery surface. He swayed, hammocked on the flat tail of the Afanc. He puttered, "Thanks again."

Lifted, he clambered onto the ledge of the pit and climbed out, while the beast below scraped at the sides and roared, roaming.

"I'll get'cha out," Winslow promised. The coast above was clear, but loud with the chirrs, croaks, and yowls of other creatures locked in similar crates all around. He huffed a breath of resolve. "I'll get'cha all out."

One by one, locks fell, legendary creatures filing free, while empty crates were kicked or pushed into the pit. Percival watched the operation curiously and hooted, as the sailor went to unlock another one, testing a few keys before the right one clicked, and the barred door squealed open.

From a cage labeled, *Great Auk*, a black-and-white bird shuffled free. Its oversized, hooked beak honked while its flipper-wings waved.

"*Not too strange*," Winslow mumbled.

Atop that crate, he unlocked another labeled, *Water Leaper*, and sprang back when a ball of steaming goo was lobbed. After he dodged the projectile, he glimpsed the gelatinous splatter on the floor, then the animal that hacked it. Two limbs fanned the webby gliders of a basketball-sized toad that flapped down. Winslow dipped to avoid the barbed tail swinging hazardously behind it.

"Not too normal…"

The Water Leaper's yellow, horned eyes moistened as its throat puffed a gurgling, phlegmy croak.

"Yeah, yer welcome."

More empty crates tumbled into the pit, creating a pseudo-staircase that Percival investigated with a sniff, setting a cautious paw on one.

A sheep-sized creature with a whiskered, wrinkled face like a miniature manatee, floppy dog-like ears, stubby elephantine feet, and a round body shelled with barnacles cautiously peered from the unlocked crate labeled, *Shore Laddie*. Where its gray skin was visible, it appeared dryly cracked, bruised, and even burned in places. The young sailor tried to coax him out fully, saying, "No one's gonna hurt ya now," but the abused creature made a fearful bleat, and retreated into the familiar shadows of its crate.

Winslow sighed, "It's okay, fella. Take yer time."

The Shore Laddie watched from the shade as a mustached pinniped called a *Sea Ape* was loosed next, barking and tromping free on wide flippers.

Then, Winslow spotted a smaller cage on the ground near the entrance of the chamber. He saw movement inside: a shimmery, dark body about the size of a terrier. When he found the right key and unlocked it, a sea snail-like animal slithered out. A young Morgawr.

Winslow sighed, confirming his earlier suspicion. "She weren't after me." He picked up the baby, strings of slime stretching. "*Uch.*" He set him on a table. "Sit... tight, alright?" The snail whistled. He looked at his hands, then wiped them on his already-destroyed vest, muttering, "*Why not,*" and continued his mission.

Soon, Winslow had to stand with his legs wide, as a sea of creatures flooded the floors and figure-eighted around him. He undid another lock to free a small, quiet, purple creature, scaled and gilled like a fish but with frog-like legs in a crudely humanoid stance and little pectoral fins in the rough semblance of webbed fingers. It waddled out with a bouncing, dance-like gait from a crate labeled, *Sea Bishop*. The pointy, hat-like shape of its head and the flowy, robe-like fins on its back gave credence to that name. It even stopped a moment to fan its right fin vertically, then horizontally in a cross-pattern, as though blessing his liberator.

"Erm… thanks," Winslow said.

Increasingly baffled, he trudged on, finding the keys that corresponded to their crates, until he arrived at those by the fighting ring. The shelled mammals with the label *Skeljaskrímsli* and the nickname *Icelandic Sea Wolves* were freed fairly easily, the malaised monsters sculling from their holds on paddlers with long, sloth-like claws. Their spiky club-tails clunked as they passed. Winslow gave them a moment to get clear before addressing the other former combatants.

Dobhar-chú, their cage read, *Irish Crocodiles*. These creatures were particularly fearsome: dog-sized otters, striped like badgers, and baring formidable fangs and claws equal to their reputed ferocity. He considered for a moment whether they were too dangerous to free, then heard the gentle hum of the Afanc. Percival climbed the improvised staircase of empty crates and hoisted himself out of the pit, roaring. In concurrence, the baby Morgawr whistled on a surface beside the dining area, where the unfinished meals left by the criminals still steamed. Winslow nodded.

The young sailor winced at the disturbing food, then swept the platters off their tables, as the hungry, tumbling mass of Irish Crocodiles snarled and yipped louder in their cage. He went back to the lock, telling himself, *"They ain't after me,"* then twisted the key.

Some time later, a lone gangster traversed the halls. It was oddly silent at first, then riotous, swelling with a collage of yips, yowls, croaks, and growls as the flickering, beastly shadows stretching over the stone were trailed by a herd of legends, shepherded by the young sailor who sat boldly above the parade, atop the Afanc's back.

Winslow tipped his chin. "Howdy."

The gangster shrieked, outcry muffled by a splattering glop of slime retched by the Water Leaper, adhering the man to the wall. The young Morgawr slithered onto the sailor's shoulder and whistled.

"Let's go."

"There ya have it..." Winslow said shakily.

Voss clapped. "Bravo, Mr. Hoffner! Kabel was right about you—what a tale!" He sat back, delighted, and pointed. "You're a regular legend hunter in the making, you know that? I feel like I'm looking in a mirror."

"Don't flatter yerself."

"*Hm.*" Voss' head dipped, shading his pyrite stare. "And there's that fabled *wit* as well... I shudder to think what could drain you of that mirth." He stood, and without need of direction, Shaull and Stokes set upon their captive once more.

"Where are they?" Stokes demanded.

"*Nowhere,*" Winslow garbled between blows.

The torture was fruitless. Eventually, Stokes stepped back while Shaull took over. He whispered to his superior, "*Ee ain't talkin', Voss.*"

The leader strolled, thinking, then stopped at a sight in the hallway: another henchman, soaked in green goo. The man's traumatized, wild eyes flicked between cohorts, as he tugged a wailing, chained animal into the chamber. Voss grinned, then answered Stokes, "Of course he isn't talking; you're hurting *him.*"

Shaull ceased the beating. Winslow muttered an inaudible taunt, words trailing when he found the Shore Laddie staring back at him, quivering under Voss' arm.

"You missed one."

The young seafarer's ice-blue stare flitted under his swollen features, darting between the soft, brown eyes of the scared, lamb-like creature, and the hand of his captor, which dipped into a pocket on his grungy, leather jacket.

Winslow strained, "What're ya...?"

"Finish the story." An ivory handle rose. The Shore Laddie squirmed.

"Wait."

The red glow of torches flashed on a blur of metal, as a spring-loaded blade flicked out from the handle.

"Wait, wait, *don't — !*"

The weapon plunged. The animal squealed. Its flailing shadow wrapped over the young seafarer's horrified face. Empty stare locked on his prisoner, Voss twisted the knife slowly. He smiled.

Winslow screamed, "Stop!"

"Finish it!" Voss frothed.

The Shore Laddie's desperate brown gaze pleaded for intercession.

Winslow's blue eyes met the creature's. He repeated his demand, but Voss ignored it. The gang leader's unhinged giddiness was spilling out of him now, flowing from a gaping grin in waves of hyenic cackles. The laughter broke only when his teeth reconnected with an ecstatic, spitting growl, as he levered his knife once more.

Winslow tried to rise. Shaull and Stokes held him in place and traded harried looks.

The Shore Laddie kicked and wailed.

Voss readied his weapon for another strike.

"I said stop!" Winslow screamed. "I'll tell ya!" His chest heaved. The blade dripped. The animal's barnacled back rose faintly with breath. Winslow nodded, "I'll tell ya," then shook his head, scowling through the firelight and promising, "It won't do ya any good, though."

Stomping to the end of the candlelit hall, Percival hooted, and Winslow dropped from his back. The great beast shook his bill with a clacking, docile warble. Winslow patted his flank and the baby Morgawr whistled on their savior's shoulder as he maneuvered through the teem of mythical runaways to the final metal door that plugged the passage. It didn't budge.

A panel beside it awaited a keycode. Winslow grumbled. He tried random numbers, bashed it with his hand, and even tried short-circuiting the device with the shock-stick to no avail. He grunted with his final attempt to wrench it open, arms dropping defeatedly, then glanced behind him at the roaring, raring Percival. With a flash of understanding, Winslow hopped out of the way.

BOOM! The metal door dented, and with a second, charging bash, it was bulled off its hinges, revealing a stretch of clear grass, then woods.

"Best solutions is usually the simplest, huh?"

Percival huffed, then howled triumphantly.

Winslow petted him.

The monsters all flowed out around him, limping and starved, but alight with ebullience. Likewise sore, but happy, the seafarer staggered behind the herd, relieved. Then, a light stepped out from the trees, and he stopped in his tracks.

Around those trees, mist crawled. Beyond those glittering spirals he could sense the ripples of water. And right up front, framed by the magic, a living shape glowed at the center of it all. The apparition waved.

The glimmers cast on Winslow's dazzled features flashed while he cycled emotions—wonder, elation, providence—before a chuckle broke free and his face settled in a look of gallantry. "Fancy seein' you here."

"The Selkie," Voss breathed.

"Aye." Winslow's eye twitched.

Voss, thoroughly engaged, handed the injured Shore Laddie over to his third henchman.

Winslow watched the exchange and read the faces of his sinister audience, then continued, "After the water spirit gathered her pals, n' I dropped off the li'l Morgawr ta be with 'is momma, I thought I was home free—till yer *guy* showed up." He nodded grudgingly at Stokes, then followed up with a smirk. "Gave me a start, so I gave 'im a shock with Shaull's zapper."

Stokes twitched, snarling.

Voss turned. "Is *that* the burning I smelled?"

"Went down like a sack o' potatoes—"

"I was standing in a puddle!" Stokes roared.

Voss snickered, then looked down, seeming to just now notice the Shore Laddie's blood on his clothes. He touched it and puttered a lower laugh, as though pleasantly surprised, then smeared the carnage deeper into his jacket.

Winslow cringed. In the midst of the tense exchange, however, he watched the bystanding henchman carry the delirious Shore Laddie out of the room to return it to its crate in the main chamber. Winslow's breathing steadied a little. His fluttering, swelled eyes chased thoughts.

Voss rubbed the red stains on his hands. "I must say, I appreciate you being so *forthcoming*."

Winslow pulled in a slow breath, then coughed and shrugged with his bound arms. "Well, like I said, them critters is gone. *Gone* gone."

"Pray tell."

"That lake," Winslow shook his head, confident, "it weren't where I came upon it the first time. This time it just... *unfolded* in the woods all a sudden, like..." He shook his head. "*Heh.* Anywho, it don't matter. The mist got real thick. N' when it parted, there weren't no sign of it." As his interrogator stood and turned, Winslow added, "I weren't kiddin' when I said they was *nowhere*." Voss' back shook, and Winslow concluded slyly, "That's right. I reckon the Selkie took them beasties somewhere that don't exist."

Voss' back rattled more, and Winslow started to smile, but his expression faded when the pattern was accompanied by a low, internal hum that pounded into tremulous laughter. Winslow frowned.

"Oh, Mr. Hoffner..." Voss rotated. His pyrite eyes shone sharply. "I'm afraid you have no *idea* what exists." He stroked the pelt on his shoulder.

Winslow dissected the action with renewed prudence, and terror.

Voss tracked the stare. "Selkies." He tutted, stained fingers sullying the spotted, white fur. "So *trusting.*"

Feeling hands wrap his shoulders at the instruction, "*Take us there,*" the young sailor rattled, "Weren't ya hearin' me? It's gone! Nowhere!"

Voss straightened his bloodied cuffs with a dismissive laugh.

Winslow gritted doggedly, "I'm tellin' ya, the lake ain't there no more —!"

"It's not a matter of *where*. It's a matter of *who*." Voss waved, and Shaull and Stokes viced Winslow's arms and wrestled him up. "And unfortunately for *you*, Mr. Hoffner, you've made yourself quite useful to me."

Hangar 19 and the Thingamajig

trappy, tan boots crossed heel-over-ankle on the dashboard, top foot bopping to the classic country rock that vibed through the crackly radio of the red pickup. Becci Hamrin reclined in the passenger seat. Warm, morning rays beaming through her open window glinted off her new, brown-tinted, gold-rimmed sunglasses. Her cream jacket and cotton scarf had been abandoned, tossed to the backseat in favor of cooler fashion: blue jeans and a white, tourist T-shirt from their stop at a visitor center in Virginia.

John Chaplain's dark coat, scarf, and gloves were tangled in a pile with hers in the back. As he shed his wintry layers, his worry had loosened a little as well. Maybe it was the fresh scents of new, mountain air, the warmer temperatures, or just the buzz of a headlong road trip. Whatever the reason, John felt eased and excited to pursue this mystery with Becci. Still, he couldn't fight all his cautious tendencies.

"That's dangerous," he mentioned, nodding to Becci's boots on the dash.

She turned, strawberry hair flipping in the gusts of the open window to drape half her face, doubly freckled from sunshine. "*This* is dangerous?" Her specs' frames sparkled with bright reflection, backlit by warm, spring tones. The corner of her grin dimpled beside her tumbling locks. She corralled them back and rested her elbow on the window frame, while a blur of verdant trees and bushes in bloom scrolled by behind her. "You remember where we're going, don't you?" The Cryptolabe swung on its chain as she leaned; she wore it like an oversized necklace now.

"Yeah," John said. "Still. Might as well be safe."

"Alright, *Dad*." She pulled her knees in and sat upright. "Happy?"

"I'm just saying. I've never driven a truck—"

"For the past couple of days you have."

"Or a vehicle this old—"

"*Vintage.*" Becci checked around her. "Custom, too. You don't see a lot of backseats in fifty-fives."

"You didn't strike me as a car person."

"I'm not. But I have four brothers who are. And an annoyingly-good memory."

John's phone buzzed beside him.

Becci touched her temples as if in psychic projection. "Coffee girl."

John went for the phone, but Becci snatched it first. "*Ehp.* That's dangerous." She checked the screen. "Winter Costello. *Yep.* Called it."

"You *do* have a good memory." John reached.

Becci scooched right. "Hands on the wheel." She swiped. "*Wow.* So many cat memes."

"Yeah, she," John sighed, "sends a lot of those."

Becci read a caption, "Hope your day is *meow't* of the ordinary!"

"Is this necessary?"

"For the story? Absolutely. I need to know where your head's at." Becci waved an invisible paragraph in the air. "A daring trip south to find an abandoned CRYPTICA outpost. A lovestruck journalist daydreaming about the belle of Brite N' Earlies..."

"You can look if you promise not to write that."

"Cool." Becci scrolled, wondering, "You two... hitting it off?"

"We're just chatting right now."

"You like her?"

"She's nice. She's talking about meeting up for coffee sometime."

"Original."

"Heh, yeah."

"Is this the future Mrs. Chaplain?"

"Oh, *geez*, c'mon." John laughed a little and shrugged. "I... dunno. I don't even know if she's my type."

"What's your type?"

John glanced at her, but before he could answer, the Cryptolabe around her neck started rattling.

Becci jolted and traded shocked looks with him, then popped the lid. The purple needle spun under its glass dome and quivered right, bulbs flashing at a reading. Her eyes chased the direction and landed on a rusted road sign.

"*Breaker Road,*" she read.

We're here, John thought. Up until now, the revelations shared in the houseboat were just part of a fantastical story. Now, the first concrete detail of that story stood before them, and a sensation of impending discovery buzzed, as John braked and pulled off. Even with his cautious driving the turn was sharp and sudden.

"Sorry," he apologized. As they swung over the serpentine road and the woods' branches interlaced above their lone vehicle to form an arboreal tunnel, John faded the music and flipped on his recorder's playback.   The fisherman's directions fuzzed through Becci's external speaker:

"Careful not ta miss Breaker Road. That'll sneak up on ya. Next part's tricky. Yer lookin' fer a sign called Clover Hill Airfield. But it's been a while. So, ya might have ta make a few laps, go with yer gut..."

The truck hummed to a roll beside a turnoff that led to a dirt road, crisscrossed with sticks and weedy overgrowth.

"Look fer somethin' obvious, like, 'No Trespassin'.'"

Scraping, twiggy branches clawed at the windows and doorframes, as John and Becci ventured down a dark, wooded path that spilled onto roadless, unruly grass, where willowy curtains draped a red sign of the predicted warning. Becci addressed the Cryptolabe and pointed.

"Dependin' on the state o' things, ya might have ta get creative with yer interpretation o' the law..."

John grunted as metal snapped under the clamp of a dull bolt cutter. Chains fell, and a viny gate was dragged open, nearly falling from its oxidized hinges. The driver's side door thumped, and the truck rumbled on, into the abandoned airfield.

"The thingamajig we're after is in Hangar 19."

"Is there a way to tell which is which?"

"Yeah, there's a big 19 on it."

"Oh."

The truck parked before the huge, semicircular façade of the dingy, metal hangar. Faded paint prominently displayed its number in stenciled, streaky characters.

The voice of Milly Matterhorn interjected on the recording, *"Ooh, a heist! This is great!"*

"This is bonkers!" her husband argued.

Winslow dithered, *"Yeah, I gots me worries too, Matterhorn. I dunno how I feels about lettin' you two go alone. If ya can hold off a week, I can come with ya."*

"We'll be fine!" Becci contended. *"We took on the Kraken. How much scarier could a simple road trip be?"*

"That's the energy!" Milly jumped in.

"What happens if they get caught? What then?" Peter countered.

"I have a couple keepsakes that can help, actually! You gifted them to me at the same time you did the Cryptolabe, Winslow. I always felt they'd come in handy…"

A briefcase squeaked open and John and Becci surfaced with the treasures. Dust spiraled as they unrolled and fanned retro coats. For John, a black one with squared shoulders. For Becci, a textured, charcoal-gray one with an elaborate, fuzzy lapel. Each had belonged to Winslow and Anna, they were told. Both had matching yellow patches with black Saturn insignias.

Thanks, Milly, John thought. He nabbed two flashlights before shutting the briefcase. As Becci smoothed her coat and scrabbled with the oversized, silver waist buckle, John smiled. "You look…" Becci raised a sly brow. He chuckled. "Groovy."

She accepted the compliment. "Thanks, J-Chap. You look…" John struck a dapper pose and she giggled; the coat was slightly too small for him. She looped the belt on her waist and strapped in. "Far out."

The pair made a wide arch to survey the massive, sealed hangar door, finding no way inside until they came upon a small, rounded-rectangular side door. In place of a knob was an immovable, metal wheel. But just before it, a lone, weathered terminal stood sentinel. John and Becci brushed away moss and dirt and scraped open a square panel cover, revealing an octagonal port. The purple glow of the Cryptolabe's bulbs all blinked in soft, fading unison when held near the interface.

Strange, John thought. The closer they came, the further he felt from his body, like he was hovering, watching the two of them wade into danger. *Is this a mistake?* Even Winslow was hesitant to let them go alone, but with their deadline approaching and Winslow off on his own mission, the journalists were gung-ho to prove themselves, pursue the truth, and protect the bay. While lost in thought, he missed a question from Becci, and he shook free. "What?"

She repeated, "I said, are you ready?"

John took a steadying breath to regain his focus. *I'm not sure if I am,* he admitted to himself, but replied, "Go for it."

Nervous, but trusting instruction, the Cryptolabe was unclipped from its chain and aligned in the panel.

"Hope this works," Becci said. She pressed.

It clicked. Clamps rose, securing the instrument and rotating it in the terminal like a key.

No turning back now, John thought.

Gears and dormant inner workings revved and rumbled awake. Even the ground beneath them shuddered, disturbed, as the wheel grumbled to the side, and the rusted, burgundy door of Hangar 19 growled and yawned open.

Smoke puffed from the exhausted terminal as the Cryptolabe unclamped. Becci blew the dust from it and clipped it back onto its chain, then winced, shaking her fingers at the heated metal.

"You good?"

"Yeah. Hot." The brassy artifact twirled, as Becci dragged her locks out from under the chain and flipped them back behind her. "C'mon."

They struck their flashlights and pressed through the musty darkness. Solid white beams sliced the black interior, illuminating boxes of secrets, shelves of odd inventions, and jarred organic samples. The final part of their interview with Winslow played in John's memory:

"Scialpi used ta call this place a 'treasure trove.' Ta me it was always more of a junkyard... Heh, one man's treasure, eh?"

This hangar was repurposed as a dumping ground for anomalies and peculiar mementos swept under the rug when the agency became spread too thin, the journalists had learned. As they ventured, their footsteps echoed into new, daunting sounds. Every stride was trailed by innumerable, clapping mimics, like their own shadows were creeping up on them.

John's beam swiped left, over mythical-looking bones with cutting, reaching, razor-like claws. He shuddered, clutching the edge of his jacket as the chilled, cavernous air licked him, then strode away.

Becci checked behind her, features lit spookily. "You scared?"

John swallowed his fear. "Nah." He shrugged, puffing his chest under the slightly-too-tight, heirloom jacket. "Ain't too bad."

"*Ain't?*"

"Uh, I mean 'not.' "

Becci giggled. "You're starting to talk like Winslow now."

John laughed. "Maybe it's the jacket?"

"Maybe." Becci eyed him, then marched ahead, hair bouncing.

John smiled back, calmer, and his beam climbed skyward to merge with the only other light source of the hangar: a gnarled, gaping hole in the roof, toothed by broken metal. In the gold rays that spilled through, motes of dust spiraled in infinity, casting grave spotlights on the hangar's unnerving centerpieces.

Glass and metal canisters of varying shapes and sizes lined the middle. Some were square and box-like, others cylindrical. All were crisscrossed with tubing that hummed and hissed breaths of cold fog. Small flickers of green shone on their panels too. Whatever little power was still fed to this abandoned place seemed to be routed there.

"Winslow didn't mention *those*," Becci breathed.

"Maybe he didn't know about them," John surmised, striding closer. "It's been decades."

"What are they?"

As John observed the strange canisters, freakish, frozen features could be seen behind the frosted glass. *Cryptids*, he realized. "They're... *monsters*."

Becci paled, stepping around for a better view. Their beams fused to graze horrific teeth, scales, claws, and inhuman eyes. John wondered if the beasts they were attached to were still alive.

The tallest container was shaped like a rounded, vertical coffin. Its only porthole of visibility was completely frosted over. Whatever was chilled within must have been massive.

John's mind reeled, boggled. *Imagine having so many monsters that you could put them in storage and forget about them.*

His light glided over a broken glass container. Inside, something foul rotted. He coughed.

"We should get what we need and get out," Becci suggested, but promptly became sidetracked by something less gruesome. "Oh, hey! Check it out!"

"What?"

She waved John over to a shelf and pointed her light. Her partner followed and found a CRYPTICA toy set. "Mint condition," she joked.

"Oh, no way." John picked it up, amazed and abuzz with an uncanny vibe, as white light wriggled over the winged, reptilian *Chupacabra* action figure and the plastic net launcher it came with—the very same from the obscure 90's commercial they'd watched in the café.

Wild, John reflected. It wasn't too long ago that something like this would've sailed right under his radar. But ever since he met Winslow, the world was becoming stranger and stranger. *Hiding in plain sight,* he remembered.

He turned at a rustling sound to see Becci rifling through a box of papers. She inspected documents and found one with a diagram on it, then folded it up and shoved it in her jacket pocket.

"This is practically enough for a story right here!" She dug more.

"You sure that's… legal?"

Becci's face scrunched. "Are you serious?"

"Never mind. Dumb question."

Becci sighed. "Look, if it makes you feel better, Winslow's Crypto-thing opened the door for us, right?"

"Yeah."

"So, this place is either a big trashcan that's fair game, or CRYPTICA's cool with letting former employees take a trip down memory lane." She went on to the next shelf. "Also, you're the one who cut the lock outside, so technically you're the trespasser."

"Oh," John nodded. "That does make me feel better."

"You're welcome," Becci giggled. On a shelf behind, her light shone on a round, metal gadget. "Is that it?"

John adjusted his glasses and stepped around to inspect the coconut-sized contraption with bent antennas. He turned it.

"I remember there was this one gizmo," Winslow had explained in the houseboat. *"This thingamajig that always did the opposite o' what the suits wanted it ta do. Which'd make it perfect fer our purposes."*

"What's it called?" John had asked.

"No clue."

"Uh, what's it look like?"

"Kinda... like a... hm... Y'know what, lemme draw ya a picture..."

John unfolded the sketch Winslow had made and compared it, then shook his head. "No." He went on to investigate the shelves with his partner, comparing similar defunct tech against the fisherman's drawing, until they came upon a table where a surplus of gizmos was stockpiled. They rummaged. "No. No..."

Becci sighed. She set a hand down and the plank wobbled, clattering the loose, metal bits stacked atop it. She frowned and backed, illuminating the object on which the improvised surface was balanced. Her face fell. "Is *that* it?"

John joined her and held up the sketch, distinct shapes overlapping. He grimaced. "Yep."

They uncovered it: a metal sphere, the size of a washing machine, pegged with odd coils in the pattern of an old sea mine and mounted via a central rod on a wide, trapezoidal base with a confounding interface of jumbled keys, dials, and switches.

"Here we go," John said, mostly to himself. Beneath the *Thingamajig*, the tines of a sluggish pallet

lifter scraped, wheezing with decent power, but squeaking down the length of the hangar on clumsy, uneven wheels.   After assuring the load was balanced, Becci stepped back to watch John's brutally-slow progression.

"Need help?"

"The controls are on the handle..." John fiddled with the triggers, motor whining. "This is as fast as it goes." He rolled past the side door, too narrow for his cargo, then pressed on for the larger hangar door ahead. He glanced back at his clunky progress and moaned, "See you in a year."

"No, no, you're..." Becci strolled. "Doing great. Looks fun actually."

"Wanna trade?"

Becci snapped her fingers. "We *are* gonna need something to secure it to the truck, aren't we?" She disappeared. "Yeah, like a bungee or something."

"Mm-hm."

John rolled as Becci explored. She returned with a tangle of ropes that she draped over the cargo, then ventured into the darkness again, while her partner snailed on.

"You're a *huge* help," he called.

"Don't mention it," she smiled, cracking an invisible whip. "Mush!"

"You're pushing it."

"Nah, that's your job, buddy."

"Wow." John tucked his tongue in his cheek. "Touché. Y'know, I'm starting to think *you're* 'Wit' and *I'm* 'Smarts.' "

"Maybe I'm both."

"I *swear* I'll turn this thing around."

"You'd never catch me!"

They shared a laugh and Becci skipped off, then perused, snapping pictures of notes and odd scribblings. Before long, she glided back to the middle section where the frozen creatures were contained, drawn either by nagging curiosity or the beguiling spotlight cast by the roof damage. In the brightness, she checked the Cryptolabe. Like the beasts, its needle, too, was frozen.

At the edge of the glow, the final container stood. Atop a dented, metal plinth, a glass cube was shattered. Its display was dark and its panel lights were dim. And inside it, the remnants of a soft egg rotted.

Becci's expression cycled from morbid fascination, to revulsion, and back again, as she leaned in, pulled her coat over her nose, and pointed her flashlight. The fragments of membrane were a muted, sickly, celadon green. Small insects buzzed on the hardened strings of amnion where the egg had petalled apart. Becci managed to get close enough to spy the faded label, *Canvey Island Monster*, before the reeking refuse overcame her cover and she gagged and backed off. Then, a small, clicking sound of activation on the Cryptolabe drew her eye.

"John…"

With the press of a green button, the rumbling of the big hangar door overwhelmed John's ears, metal rising slowly, squealing like nails on a chalkboard, and flaking dirt, webs, and leaves. He spat away dust, then finally rolled his jangling cargo outside. After a wheezing, hydraulic lift and a gawky transfer, he managed to get the hefty mechanism onto the bed, cover it partway with an old tarp, and begin stringing it with rope.

He pulled on a knot, checking its strength, then called, "Hey Becci, I think we're good to go."

No response. Becci heard the fractured echo of her partner's call, but it faded, as her light grazed something strange, standing rigid in the shadows. Taxidermy?

Across the way, John turned. The hangar door was still rumbling the rest of the way open. *She probably can't hear me*, he reasoned. "Becci?" He ventured back in and saw her faint shape outlined in gold in the spotlight cast from the hole in the roof.

Becci edged closer to the shape, and saw teeth drip.

John stepped under the rattling, reeling passage and squinted. His partner was transfixed by something unseen. "We can—"

"JOHN!" she screamed, as a horrifying appendage slung from the black and grappled her.

John's heart thundered and eyes shot wide, as his partner was reeled into the shadows, disappearing.

He shouted her name and ran, adrenaline glazing his muscles. He couldn't feel his feet hit the floor. The sounds of his sprint carried, however, pounding under the echo of Becci's horrified wails which warped and blended with those of Hangar 19's rusted, weary door shrilling at the height of its draw, as metal folded against metal and dragged over the roof damage, grating until something snapped.

"Whoa!" John skidded. New debris loosed from the puncture above and a heavy, broken slab meteored down, crashing on the spot where Becci had stood.

When the din faded, the hisses of busted tubing and crackles of destroyed, sparking electronics pierced the wounded air. John coughed and staggered, shaken. A whipping cord dangled as the hangar door slumped to reverse its progress, hanging half-closed behind him with only a rectangle of natural light on the floor. The rest of the space was either solid darkness or dimly hued crimson by the warning lights of failing systems. Becci's left-behind flashlight flickered into an invisible corner of the hangar, and John could hear her voice ring out for him again. He ran after it; whether the call was new, echoed, or a pulse of instinct he wasn't sure, but it led him to a shadowy form, hunching by a woozy Becci.

"Hey!" he yelled. A scaly body rotated. Glowing, white ovals struck him. He balked, then charged, swinging his flashlight and spooking the hidden horror. It sprang off and he chased it for a few more steps, then helped Becci to her feet. "You alright?"

She nodded groggily, "*Yeah*," getting steady. "What *was* that?"

"I dunno."

The hangar howled with a blend of threatening noises.

"I don't think we should stick around to find out though."

John helped her along as they made the cautious sneak down the length of Hangar 19, passing whistling, busted machinery and the pile of roofing which had crashed there. Becci blanched.

"I'd have been a goner," she said.

John traced the fall to where the door had folded over the hole in the ceiling. He gulped at a pulse of guilt that locked in his chest, then spilled over into his mind with a flood of haunting scenarios. He didn't realize how tight he was holding her until she touched his hand, and the color returned to his skin. He breathed.

That thing snagged her just in time, John realized. He wondered what the creature was, and as if on cue, his answer sprang and landed in the light of the half-open hangar door. They screamed, but the fearsome shape seemed preoccupied, and when they followed the shadow they found it connected to a far less threatening source.

About two feet-tall and covered in shimmery, teal scales, a being that looked like a walking anglerfish snuffled at the open air. A single antenna with a glowing lure bobbed above her huge, oval eyes, as a fleshy throat puffed, frog-like, and uttered a soft chatter through a jaw underbitten with needly, tapping teeth.

John and Becci kept their distance.

"That must be what hatched from the egg," Becci realized. The Canvey Island Monster crouched and prowled toward a bird that had flown in to roost on a beam on the inside of the lapsing door. "How'd it survive in here so long?"

"How'd it manage to pull you across the whole hangar?"

A prehensile tongue launched from the beast's mouth and snatched the bird off its perch, leaving only a puff of feathers behind. The journalists grimaced.

"I guess that's how," Becci said, then frowned. "And did you just call me fat?"

The struck door rumbled and tottered, then slammed the rest of the way shut. The animal croaked, scampering back into the darkness.

"*Great,*" John mumbled. The slapping of the little creature's feet echoed, distant, as he went to the control to lift the door. It wouldn't budge. *This whole place is out to get us.*

The Cryptolabe rattled. Becci consulted the direction of its needle, then tugged her partner's elbow to get his attention and pointed. John froze.

With the hangar door shut, the roof damage was exposed again. But this time, its spotlight shone on the large, vertical coffin-shaped container. The porthole was thawed, and its hatch was open.

They strafed along the walls.

"*We gotta go,*" John shuddered.

Fog spilled from the pierced tubing and rolled out of the broken seal of the containment unit. Then, frosty, spindly fingers reached free and clawed the edge of the lid. A gurgling, alien warble followed.

"*Go go go.*"

They made a break for the only other exit—the side door—snaking around the precarious towers of junk and ducking behind shelves, as the new mystery hobbled free on tapping, scratching talons. In between columns, John glimpsed pieces of it: leathery flaps, hooked claws. They squeezed past another stack of gizmos.

Almost there, John thought.

From the tower of junk, a loose item tumbled out and fell. *No...* John caught it. Becci nodded, impressed, but her relief faded when the loud bleep of a notification sounded from John's phone. John cringed and went to silence it, while the Cryptolabe around Becci's neck rattled.

In the shadows, the slapping of small, webbed feet drew near, halting just beyond the edge of visible light. It was the Canvey Island Monster. Its eyes, antenna, and mouth were glowing, intensifying with a low, foreboding, clicky growl.

John fumbled with his phone to change his settings and found the latest message from Winter: a picture of a disheveled, orange tabby, shrugging, captioned, *Are You Fur Real?*

John panicked. *This is the last thing I'm ever going to see, isn't it?*

He and Becci tried to back away as the hangar thrummed with a collage of strange noises. Some of the contraptions activated on their own, including the fallen, rectangular gadget John had managed to catch; its dual antennae sparked wildly. On a shelf above, another discarded, miniature contraption with a propeller-like module began to spin, possessed, before toppling and bashing into the buttons of a stowed reel-to-reel recorder, setting its dusty tape into motion. Its distorted, crackly introduction seemed to suggest it was once a training tape for new agents. But in its current condition, the jumbled voices it played only narrated the miasma of terror.

The purple needle was going haywire now. The surrounding bulbs flashed chaotically with the intensifying white glow of the Canvey Island Monster's forewarning eyes.

Becci gasped as the Cryptolabe swung on its chain and stood on end, magnetized. Her neck twitched in fear as the chain pulled taut on her skin and the pendant quivered in midair, pointing.

The Canvey Island Monster's stare lit up like flares, as the shadows behind it seemed to solidify and fan in the living outline of massive, bat-like wings. And hovering within the dark shape, nearly nine feet off the ground, a subsequent pair of enormous, saucer-sized eyes ignited, red.

Out of the Dark

mid chaotic fits of rebelling electronics, a distorted voice hummed from the animated reel-to-reel. The words it played seemed to close in on the backstepping journalists, and the booming tone chilled them when they recognized to whom it belonged.

"Tell me, new recruits, what is it that you fear?" the recorded voice of Giuseppe Scialpi exacted. *"That you're in the wrong calling? Lost? Or, is it that you have found yourself* exactly *where you're meant to be?"*

Lights flickered. Thawing frost dribbled down the claw-tipped ends of pale, leathery wings. With one of its gray glider-arms it draped itself in a rigid, vampiric pose, then hobbled. Raptor-like talons— five per foot, arranged like inward-facing hooks— gashed the shrieking concrete as the creature uttered chattering howls that reverberated through the metal labyrinth like demented drums and broken horns.

"*I have news for you,*" Scialpi's voice returned. "*Sooner or later, we all face that which we fear the most.*"

The monster stood head and shoulders above the journalists. That was, if it had a head, or shoulders. Its eyes looked almost fused to the spot where its chest would be. It wasn't until it shambled into the sparking luminance cast from a frayed, swinging cord that its features became clearer. Its visage was that of a hunching gargoyle. Huge eyes dominated its mouthless skull, which swiveled on a wreath of pulsating, gill-like organs from which its haunting susurrations fluted, and behind, the barb of a whip-like tail slashed the air. Seconds felt like eternities to John. He was paralyzed by its stare, unsure what family of animal on Earth could possibly have shared heritage with the horror.

The luminous eyes of both cryptids intensified. In response, exposed wiring around them arced. Then, the antique, rectangular gizmo John forgot he'd been clutching superheated.

"*Ah!*" he winced, chucking it to hold his burn, then jumping in shock when the device suddenly exploded with a smoky, plasmatic, purple blast, toppling a shelving unit between them and the creatures, and igniting the fury of the taller beast.

"What the – ?"

"Come on!" Becci grabbed John's elbow and pulled him into motion, racing down the opposite way and initiating a chase. As they sprinted, the crawl of mechanisms and whipping, broken cables above joined the eerie orchestra with sounds faintly akin to untuned violins.

The pair clambered down the crimson-lit path, past the other frozen atrocities, as haywire machines were felled or flung. When their pursuer neared, the screens beside them started to flicker with green static, and the warped voices of recorded log entries crackled under the distortion:

"Now, stay focused, son. This one is unpredictable." An electric hiss. *"Facinating… Look here, the K-field readings are –"* A roar of static. *"Call Brehmer! The inhibitor isn't wor –!"* Shrieking experimentation. Beastly yowls to match the creature's. *"Manta-Man continues to exhibit unstable –"* Crackling distortion. A withered voice lamenting, *"What have we done?"* Another howl, this one from behind.

The journalists screamed and dodged a swiping claw that sent an avalanche of inventions battering over them, knocking them to the floor. John armed himself with one of the gadgets and surfaced from the pile with a bulky net launcher — the real-life equivalent of that from the toy commercial. *Huh. What are the odds?* he thought. He faced down the monster and pulled the trigger. But the central rail slid, entangled with its own projectile, and detached, clanging over the floor; each clunky component dropping and dismantling the next.

"Wow."

The half-frozen Manta-Man tripped up for a moment on the web of netting as it warbled and twitched at a jolt from a wiry, metal implant at the base of its head.

Good enough, John decided. He helped up Becci and they made a mad dash for the glow of the side door, bursting through. They were home free it seemed, but John skidded to a stop, hands on the door, turning back.

"What're you doing?" Becci yelled.

The Canvey Island Monster was bouncing for freedom as well, similarly spooked by the newly-unleashed fiend. John watched the little lantern atop her head swerve through the darkness like an evasive firefly.

John braced. The tiny creature's intercession had saved Becci from the falling debris earlier, he remembered.

He heard Becci holler again, as the crimson searchlight-eyes of the horrifying Manta-Man struck him. John winced in their menacing glow, his muscles locking. The monster's wings were still too frosted for takeoff, but the flaps provided a galloping, gliding sprint that nearly overtook the race. John swallowed. He held the door open a second longer.

CRASH! Feeling wind on his legs and sensing a blue blur spring by, John slammed the hatch shut on reflex, the locking wheel rotating with a hefty *clunk* before a gonging pound hammered from the other side. John dropped and felt his heartbeat thumping in his ears as he looked left, seeing the tall grass sway. He smiled.

Becci swatted his shoulder. "Way to play up the suspense," she panted.

John nodded with a breathless laugh.

"What were you waiting for?"

He was about to explain, but the sound of inhuman wails and a denting slam on the hangar wall cut him off.

Becci jogged. "Y'know what? We can talk about it in the truck."

"Sounds good," John agreed.

The red pickup's open doors welcomed them. Becci jumped behind the wheel, John sat passenger, and the pair absconded with their mysterious cargo back onto Breaker Road.

Hangar 19 loomed above their narrow escape, while the howling rage of the Manta-Man rolled and whorled within its walls, then spiraled high and spouted through the jagged, damaged roof.

As the pickup hummed onto the highway, John and Becci sat in tense silence, blank features held straight ahead on the empty stretch of road and the flickers of green countryside scrolling beside it. Each was trying to work out what had happened. Neither gathered enough sense to initiate the discussion.

Becci's fingers tapped on the wheel. She smiled awkwardly. "Music?"

"Yeah, music's good."

Becci turned the dial, scanning to a calmer station, and landing on a soothing, R&B tune.

John eased into the passenger seat and sighed in unison with Becci. They laughed a little at their synchronicity. John took a slow breath and held it, feeling his heartbeat settle, then exhaled slowly. *It's alright,* he told himself. He peered through the rectangular back window to see the fluttering tarp that partly concealed their find. *We did it.*

In the backseat, his jacket and scarf were entangled with Becci's in a pile. In a few days they'd need them again. He smiled. The truck rumbled, and he turned back. A sleeve moved.

He didn't detect the motion at first. He started to rest his eyes, then shot up again with a double-take, discovering, in tandem with the beats of the radio, a rising antenna bobbing free from the folds of clothing. The Canvey Island Monster pushed out and croaked.

"Becci—?"

"Hm?"

The cryptid bounced out.

"*Whoa!* What in the—?" Becci wrestled the wheel as the creature rebounded, backflipping, frontflipping, and vaulting off the cushions and windows of the backseat in a springy dance.

"Did you let it in?"

"What? No. I got in at the same time you did. *You're* the one who let it out of the hangar—"

"I-I didn't want to take it *with* us though, I just—"

The monster's eyes, mouth, and lure lit up suddenly, flashing off the rearview mirror and spotting Becci's vision.

"*AH!*"

John reached to wrench the wheel, but a bashing gnarl of squealing metal pierced the madness, as the truck tipped diagonal. Then, its left tires lifted off the street. The side of the truck was hooked by the talons of the Manta-Man.

Becci shrieked, "Are you serious?!"

The gill-like structures on its neck quavered with a pulse-pounding howl that vibrated the truck, then warbled with a jolt when the corded implant sparked.

Their yells and Becci's hammering on the glass weren't enough to dissuade the dreadful apparition, but when its haunting eyes spied an oncoming vehicle in the opposite lane, it scraped free, dropping John and Becci's squeaking, straining ride to gust high in evasion, leaving behind enormous, whistling clawmarks in the steel.

The oncoming sedan skidded and braked off onto the shoulder; John caught a flash of the occupants' stunned expressions as they sped by.

He checked the skies again, then exclaimed, "Gun it!"

"I am—*Ach!*" The Cryptolabe spun on its chain and went chokingly taut against Becci's throat, pendant magnetized backward. The pursuing entity's eyes were glowing brighter, highlighting the journalists' fearful faces and their tiny, croaking passenger with horrid, crimson tones. John gaped; from this angle, the Manta-Man looked like a sentient shadow, swimming through the air, with only its blood-colored stare alit in hypnotizing intensity.

The floating, tugging Cryptolabe's inner bulbs flashed a wild purple through its seam. John unlooped the chain from Becci's neck. She panted, and the device flew out of John's grasp to *clunk* against the window, adhered.

"You alright?"

"*Peachy!*" Becci pierced.

John's ears rang. "Sorry—"

"We gotta do something soon, or—"

THOOM! The Manta-Man hooked the sides of the truck's bed and flapped, lifting.

"*Whoa!*" John and Becci shouted.

The glass of the back window cracked. The Manta-Man howled and hoisted. The engine graveled a desperate roar, as the front grille scraped the road and shot sparks. In the chaos, John's recorder skipped to an earlier timecode and activated:

"*We'll be fine!*" Becci's voice played on the speaker. "*We took on the Kraken. How much scarier could a simple road trip be?*"

"Ah, shuttup! Whadda *you* know?!" Becci screamed at her past self.

A hard bash sent the journalists tossing forward. John grunted against the dash, the radio cycling stations with the impact.

A flash went off in the backseat. The radio whirred, and the Manta-Man recoiled at a shock from the implant on its neck, dropping them. The red pickup jounced and the back window shattered, the magnetized Cryptolabe soaring through. John followed the whistling breezes to the damage, throat bobbing, then saw the Cryptolabe's chain tangled up in the pegs of the Thingamagig.

If Hangar 19 was Winslow's idea of a junkyard, the Manta-Man was a fitting junkyard dog. What it wanted, if anything, John couldn't figure, but the way it reacted to the scanning of the radio and the glow of the Canvey Island Monster gave him an idea. John dialed, scrolling through stations.

"What are you doing?"

John shrugged, watching for reactions from the creature. "Something," John said. *I hope.* He spun the knob. Nothing. He switched frequencies and scanned, until white noise stormed in the speakers. The Manta-Man was beside them again, haunting stare fixated, implant jolting it with a mad twitch.

"Leave us alone!" Becci wailed.

In the backseat, the Canvey Island Monster's eyes, mouth, and lure lit up again, the sounds of the radio warping in unison with her growing, white glow and low, clicky growl. John's phone pixilated with a jumble of colored bars and distorted cat pictures. The external speaker jostled, playing other parts of the interview. The fisherman's voice fuzzed through, jumping:

"Didn't know — Di-Didn't know — None of 'em were exactly sure what it was — wha-what it was afore they started foolin' with it — foolin' ... They was jottin' stuff down n' guessin' — K-fields — then followin' it like it was fact — fact... like it wasn't all boohockey."

The journalists reeled and cried at the insane clamor of voices and crazed machines. The truck's hazard lights blinked and windshield wipers went off. Even the long-dormant machine they hauled intercepted a phantom charge from the air, then revved, hummed, and began rotating on its rod. The ropes that secured it started to snap.

" — like it wa — like it wasn't all boohockey... boo — "

The Manta-Man swooped. The journalists screamed.

At the apex of the little beast's shine, its blinding luminescence flashed. The chugging Thingamajig did too, spinning rapidly, then pulsing out a rippling shockwave, followed by a stray bolt that arced, charred the chassis, fried the radio, and connected with the implant on their attacker's neck.

The Manta-Man let out an electrified yowl, then spasmed and fell, as the device combusted.

"Yes!" Becci exulted.

The truck puttered, slowing, while the shape of the monster shook and rose in the field behind them, clawing off the destroyed implant.

"No. Nonono…" Becci tried to start the truck again.

The Canvey Island Monster was out cold in the backseat, little chest rising. John's eyes darted. The Manta-Man opened its wings.

Becci raved, "No, you've gotta be kidding me. Come on!" She hammered the dash, and the truck roared alive. Her wild, olivine eyes looked it over for a half-second, before her hands clambered for the wheel. "Thank you." She drove.

But the Manta-Man wasn't far behind. He galloped into a gliding sprint as Becci muttered praise to the vehicle, then switched to harried curses when the monster caught up in no time.

Inexplicably, John felt calmer in the cryptid's presence this time. And when the flying behemoth caught up and swiveled his head with owl-like curiosity through the passenger-side window, his red eyes had somehow softened to more of a warm violet hue. The entity cocked his head again, then took off vertically.

Becci panted, harried, then whispered to the sputtering truck again, "*Thank you.*"

John and Becci sat at a picnic table on the lawn of a roadside dive called *Peggy's Old Dominion Soda Parlor and Creamery*. John sipped a root beer float and Becci licked spoonfuls of ice cream in exhausted, traumatized silence under the shade of a humongous swirly cone sculpture—the biggest in the world, according to its plaque.

A kind, curly-haired woman dropped off extra napkins. "Can I get y'all anythin' else?"

"No, we're good," John replied. "Thanks, Deb."

"Sure thing, hun." She shielded her eyes from the sun and crooned, "*Aw,* is that your puppy?"

Becci swallowed.

John looked to see the groggy Canvey Island Monster rising from her nap in the backseat, cocooned in their pile of coats. Partly-obscured by laundry, the creature waddled up to the half-open window and snuffed steam on the smudgy glass.

"Can I pet her?"

"No," John said quickly.

Deb covered her chest.

He explained, "She's… weird."

The monster made a clicky croak and licked the window.

"*O…kay.*" Deb looked next at the giant machine in the bed. "Huh."

The journalists exchanged glances.

Deb pointed. "Speakin' of weird, whatcha haulin' there?"

Becci pretended to be distracted, picking a small, yellow, buttercup flower from the weeds at her feet and twirling it until she crafted an answer. "Art," she lied.

"Oh…" Deb murmured.

Becci tucked the buttercup behind her ear with feigned naïveté, then took a slow, worried spoonful from her sundae, as she and John awaited inevitable further questioning.

But to their relief, Deb's cheeks dimpled genially. "That's nice." She waved. "Holler if ya need me, okay?"

Once she was gone, Becci sighed, trying to relax.

"Hey, great driving back there," John said.

"*Pssh.*" Becci rolled her eyes. "More like hanging on for dear life. You really came in clutch with the radio thing. How'd you figure that out?"

"Luck," John admitted, then nodded to the Canvey Island Monster in the truck. "I think she had something to do with it too."

The little creature pressed on the window again, sniffing. Outside, a bird pecked at the ground. When John noticed, he scooped up a couple chicken strips from his plate and told Becci he'd be back.

As he slipped food to the monstrous stowaway in the backseat, a voice made him turn and block the window:

"Ya should be up n' runnin' now," a husky man with an impressive, brown beard shut the hood of the truck and wiped his hands on a rag. He smiled.

"I'd take 'er into the shop just to be safe, though. Looks like she was struck by lightning in there!"

"Will do. Thank you, Huell." John reached for his wallet.

"Ah, no need for that." Huell waved away the payment, hooking his thumbs on the straps of his overalls.

"You sure?" John asked. "I already had it converted. Might as well go to a good guy."

"It's no trouble. Saw your plates. What brings ya all the way down here? Honeymoonin'?"

"Huh? No. Just, uh…" John glanced at Becci, then grinned. "Just an adventure."

"Hm." Huell's beard puffed as he nodded in approval. "Nothin' wrong with that."

As the Good Samaritan left and John returned to Becci, the Canvey Island Monster sniffed and explored the truck. When her glowing lure bobbed near the recorder, it activated, playing Winslow's voice on the speaker:

"K-fields… I reckon there's somethin' to 'em. Whether the suits' science was the best way ta uncover it, I ain't so sure. If ya ask me, there's more magic in the world than we realize…"

John observed the Canvey Island Monster exploring the truck and asked Becci, "What are we gonna do with her?"

"What do you mean?"

"I mean, we can't just free her; she's never been outside—and we don't know enough about her natural environment either. Is it the ocean? The swamp?" Becci licked her spoon, as John rambled. "But we can't really *keep* her either, can we—?"

"I love her," Becci interjected.

John paused. "Uh, okay…"

As Becci stared at the truck, her eyes flashed. John asked what she was thinking, and she revealed, "My annoyingly-good memory is remembering something." When John leaned in for elaboration, she said, "Didn't Winslow mention that he stole that one agent's truck back in the day?"

John searched his mind, then said, "Yeah, I think so… but what does—?"

Becci pointed with her spoon. "Think that's the truck?"

John thought. "No… no way." He looked behind him at the classic vehicle, then swallowed and paled. "Maybe."

Becci grinned.

"What?"

"Nothing."

"What?"

She let out a punchy, squeaking laugh. "I'm just imagining us trying to cross the border with an exotic animal and a machine that looks like a bomb..." she held her ribs, "in a *stolen* truck!"

John got harried, eyes widening. "Yeah. Me too. It's not funny."

"It's a little funny."

"How is it funny?"

" 'Cause I think we're gonna make it somehow. And it'll be a hilarious story when we do."

John smiled. "No, we're both getting arrested for sure." He stood and offered a hand. "Ready to get out of here?"

"Yeah." Becci dropped her spoon in her empty cup, then quipped, "Might as well while it's *calm*, right? I've had enough close calls for today."

As they got up to leave, something tore through the sky. Deb, Huell, and other murmuring watchers got up to shade their eyes and stare too. John and Becci squinted as their hair flipped wildly in the gusts. Above, black helicopters chopped the clouds in low formation, racing in the direction to which the Manta-Man had escaped.

John and Becci gawped high, then to each other.

"Y'know what?" Becci followed up. "If anyone asks, we were never in Appalachia."

Always

emory's a bit like poetry, ain't it, Anna?" the sailor mused. "The way it's jogged, like the past is... *rhymin'* with the present all a sudden. So, ya gives it a couple reads through ta gather the full meanin'—see what life is tryin' ta teach ya." He rowed, sniffed, and nodded. "That's why I thinks we learn the most about ourselves at the best n' hardest times in our lives. Them's the times we tell stories about."

The small rowboat bobbed through sapphire swells, while the matching, dazzling eyes of Anna Meria Lough twinkled at her husband.

He went on, "Of late, I've felt like I've been on a scavenger hunt... tryin' ta find all the right memories ta piece t'gether this mystery. Ta tell the *whole* story. I hope yer still with me, darlin'."

She pretended to snore.

He laughed with her. "Thanks a lot."

"I'm jokin'," she giggled. "I'm always with ye. I'm not goin' anywhere."

He smiled.

Morning rays shimmered on her outline. In the sky, the sun and moon were both awake. The feathery streaks of cirrus that tempered them looked like roseate drapery, and the breeze that drew those cloudy curtains smelled of nighttime chill, dew, and lake water. The sailor breathed it all in. The feeling coated his locking throat. He swallowed. He knew from where it came.

Above, the dreamy sky dusked. Fiery tones blended with the cold glow of night, as the sun and moon seemed to merge into a single shape, and a hauntingly-familiar celestial event.

Anna looked worried.

Winslow told her, "It'll be alright."

Then, a voice from the past cut in: *"Where do you think you are, Mr. Hoffner?"*

Winslow Hoffner's knees knocked achingly on the gonging metal of Voss' cold rowboat. He shivered and gaped at the scene, ruled over by the looming presence of a blood moon. Though his vision was nearly as clouded as the twinkling, thick fog that hung over those waters, the location was unmistakeable: Misty Lake.

On his forehead, the pounding pains of fatigue, torture, and terror returned to merge with the fresh stings of a rough and slamming car ride to the edge of that fabled lake. Here it was. It was back again. The sailor panted and struggled against the ties on his wrists.

"Speechless," Voss hissed, turning to the thugs behind him with a creeping, wide smile. "*That's* a good sign."

Shaull and Stokes chortled in agreement.

"Row."

They hushed and hurried into motion.

Armed men prowled the perimeter at the water's edge and took aim at the rippling surface, some with tranquilizer guns, others with rifles. Behind them, trucks were stacked with empty crates, and a couple other boats flowed alongside them in a tight V-formation.

They'd have their work cut out for them to haul back every beast, but whenever questioned on the logistics of such a task, Voss would invoke the legend of the Selkie, attesting that a single pelt from such a creature would match the value of all their living cargo, and then some. And, he'd add, if the worth of a *pelt* was so staggeringly high, that of a living specimen would be all the more incalculable. Shaull and Stokes were baffled by the assertion, but rowed on nonetheless.

Winslow's dry throat was choked by dread as he watched the skulking gangsters on the shoreline and felt the sneering, dark intent of those fiends on the flanking boats. He scowled at the mishmash of hired goons — some were rough and ragged, others clean and pressed — villains from all walks of life and all corners, all looking to drain the world of its wonders for a paycheck.

How did this happen? Despite his best efforts to lead the gangsters astray, they arrived there just the same. How they came upon the uncharted, vanishing lake, and what force had willed it to appear again Winslow couldn't fathom. He breathed, and shut his stinging eyes. He hoped he was dreaming. He even hoped, for a moment, that everything that had happened to him on these far-flung voyages was a delusion—even at the cost of the great revelry he'd felt in the company of true magic. Because, he decided: real or not, at least those wonders would be safe.

But, no. No matter how hard he shut his eyes, he awoke to this same moment, over and over. Floating on the same lake beneath the same blood moon, with a rising, loaded weapon aimed at him. *This* was real.

"*Turn back...*" Winslow graveled, pained.

Voss ignored his plea, gestured with the gun, and goaded, "Go ahead, Mr. Hoffner. Cry out for your monsters."

Winslow's icy stare, masked by bruises, honed on his captor. At his silence, he was butted by the handle of the gun. His jaw rang on the rim of the metal boat, and a drop of his blood blipped into the water.

Wind chilled, and the soft glow of firefly-lights dancing in the fog stretched into angry, burning shapes, as Winslow was wrenched up by the vicing grip of Voss.

"I *won't* ask again."

The sailor spat, and scoffed, "*Then don't.*"

Voss smiled. When a splash was heard, he released his hold on Winslow and turned. The muzzles of a dozen guns did the same, clamoring for the source of the sound. But only a mundane frog was found, puffing atop a lily pad. It croaked.

Winslow panted.

With a flash of rage, Shaull turned and growled, "He lied to us. He played you for a fool, Voss—"

Crack! Stokes silenced him with a fist. "You watch your mouth!" he frothed.

Shaull roared and shoved him back. "Look around, you *dolt!* It's desolate. This isn't a '*vanishing lake.*' There are no monsters here." Three sets of fiendish eyes leered on the wounded, young seafarer shivering at the prow. Shaull wiped his mouth and continued, scowling, "He made it up. He played along to save his own skin."

Winslow checked the empty waters, wondering if his hopes had been answered. He puffed a laugh through his nose.

"Is…" Voss crept closer, pyrite eyes at first filled with rage and betrayal, then blanking, "this true?" He slapped him. "*Huh?*" He laughed insanely, then reigned in his spitting madness with a jittery breath, stroking the pelt on his shoulder. "You… *realize* I'd have no use for you otherwise, don't you?" Shaull and Stokes shrank as far back as they could in the boat as their fiendish leader pressed, demanding to know, "Are the monsters here, or *not?*"

When Winslow answered only with a sneer, he was beaten again, twisting to face the rippling lake. Shadows moved beneath the surface, following a spiral of howls. Perhaps wind, perhaps something else.

Then, the cocking gun clicked.

"Which is it?"

Winslow's stare hovered, following a pattern of dark blots in the lake to the draping withes of a lone willow on the bank. Its branches nodded, and his eyes glinted, while chilled, spectral vapors whooshed in to obscure the other flanking boats. The hapless voices of those who manned the vessels somehow distorted in the smothering fog.

Winslow's captors looked around, suddenly alone in eerie blankness, as their prisoner turned to face them down.

The revolver aimed. Voss' finger touched the trigger.

Winslow's eyes narrowed, aglint as the moon, sharp, steadied, and certain. His bruised lip curled above his bloodstained, blond beard, and he answered:

"Aye… there be monsters."

Roaring jaws ripped from the lake. The gun thundered but missed its mark when Voss' hand and forearm disappeared in the toothy maw of the breeching Afanc, and with a twisting tear and popping snap, it severed.

The man screamed, holding an empty joint. The boat threw, and amid the lingering ringing and wild, splashing calamity, the young seafarer leapt from the springing boat.

As though rising to meet his shoes, the shelled backs of Sea Wolves surfaced. With his hands bound, Winslow hopscotched on the sturdy armor of the buoyant mammals, each mouth snapping open one by one with activated ferocity and assailing the poachers, bashing them off their boats, where an ambush of Irish Crocodiles lay in wait. The hound-sized otters yipped and spiraled like furry piranhas on the misfortunate souls.

Behind the sailor's daring escape, swirling mist burst with cloaked gunshots, flaring like lightning in a storm cloud. Screaming faces appeared in vapory portals for brief moments as claws, teeth, tail-clubs, and barbs beset them. Shaull and Stokes gurgled yells as their boat flipped, and they were ravaged and dragged under.

Ahead of them, Voss thrashed after their escapee, kicking the desperate faces of his cohorts backward into the tumbling, biting brood, before he flailed his way forward.

A bullet from the flurry of unloading rifles grazed Winslow's ribs. He hollered and flung into the water. All around wove the forms of legends. Flashes of fangs and claws. Plumes of red. Streaks of bullets zipping through. Muffled shouts and underwater roars.

He kicked, grunting bubbles, as blood spilled from his side, the muscles of his bound arms burning, and the heavy drag of his clothes limiting advancement. Then, something snipped the bonds on his wrists.

Biting him free, then torpedoing before him, an agile seal appeared. Winslow hovered, as the animal's head made a dipping motion. She flipped, showing a back fin that still bore the jagged scar from the poacher's trap.

The seal made a spin and flapped for the surface. Winslow blinked underwater, nearly forgetting he needed to breathe. When his lungs burned, he bubbled and pulled, but before long, a leathery surface rose to cradle him, and push him to air.

Winslow lay on the bill of the Afanc. He caught the soft, brown eyes of his grunting companion.

"Thanks, Percy," he whispered through a trickle of lake water on his lips, as more flowed off his back, and the beast stomped onto land, carrying him toward light.

In the lake beyond, Winslow glimpsed the maimed figure of Voss attempting to paddle after him, screaming his name. He pulled, but the weight of his waterlogged, leather jacket dragged him deeper. The fury on his face melted a moment when a white glow from the woods washed over him.

The figure from whom it shined gestured.

"NOOO!!!" Voss erupted, as beasts descended, shimmering swirls of phantasmal fog covered him, the woods folded over itself like origami, and Misty Lake vanished without a trace.

I had a hard time grapplin' with what really happened. Couldn't hardly grasp any of it back then. N' now, lookin' back, pickin' it all apart... I guess it took all this distance n' time ta see what it truly meant.

Winslow shot up, gasping and coughing, body simmering with leftover adrenaline and dread, until the warmth of his company softened his nerves and summoned relief. A woman made of light sang lullabies to the Afanc, who rested his huge, weary bill on the water spirit's shining lap.

The nighttime serenade was joined by other hidden performers, likely of insectoid or amphibian origin, but like nothing Winslow had ever heard. They sounded like tiny harpists, fluters, violinists, and the gentle thrums of angelic instruments yet imagined. The Afanc breathed tiredly, a dribble of noble blood streaming from a wound in the roof of his top bill.

"*Aw, Percy...*" Winslow choked, hand hovering over the injury.

Percival blinked serenely and huffed, wet nostrils blowing his freer's teary, ashen features.

"Ya did good," he assured, free hand gripping the bleeding bullet wound over his ribs.

Percival nosed him.

"Yeah, this one's real," Winslow smiled. "We'll be alright, though."

Another, ethereal hand flowed by the sailor's. The Selkie hummed soothing tones, as melodies played in the swaying withes of the lone willow, singing backup for the loveliest voice imaginable.

Up until now, I hadn't the foggiest idea what this thing was — what energy was guidin' me all this time. Sure, everyone had a theory. Some o' the suits tied it ta "K-fields." Some o' me closest pals called it a "charm." As fer me...

The young seafarer's throat bobbed, as he beheld truth in the light, felt peace in the spirit's song, and identified a pulse of buzzing, hopeful energy that unified with a swelling sensation of impending adventure.

Tears blurred his vision, but the Selkie's beauty shined through all the same, as her stunning vibrance dimmed to fair, human flesh, and her floating hair met gravity again, tumbling over her shoulders in familiar, darling, crimson waves— unmistakable—framing the smile of a girl he met in a seaside, Scottish pub. The most remarkable woman he'd ever known.

I thinks it's love.

Rocking on their small, wooden rowboat, Winslow clapped his Journal of Curiosities shut, as his wife intertwined with him in repose, crossing her legs over his lap. Anna's soft fingertips traced his torso to the bullet scar on his ribs. Likewise, her husband's hand flowed along her fair legs to the jagged scar on her right ankle.

"After all that chaos, I found ya… You n' me ran back ta the hideout soon as we could ta free the Shore Laddie, 'member? Ran inta the suits fer the first time, then. Turned out some o' the poachers used ta run with 'em afore they went rogue. Others were ex-PRIMAL. Blew the lid offa them poachers' operation afore CRYPTICA had the chance ta. One thing led ta another n' the suits offered us a gig."

"The rest is history."

"Aye, it's quite a story," Winslow laughed in near disbelief at the outcome. "Amazin' how it all turned out. Sometimes I still have ta pinch meself ta make sure I ain't dreamin'."

"That's 'cause ye tell it so well."

Winslow chuckled. As their small vessel floated in a lulling sway, he reflected, "They say truth is found in the stories we tell. N' tellin' them stories is the way we find them truths."

"Who's *they*?" Anna asked.

"Well… me!" Winslow snorted. "Other folks too, I s'pose. I'm sure they's out there."

"Tellin' tales tae figure why they were tellin' tales in the first place?"

"Aye! Exactly. See? You n' me. That's *they*."

His lady giggled.

Birdsong heralded the handsome pair as they floated in eternity. Winslow breathed in every moment, not wanting it to end, then told her, "Ya saved me life. Ya *changed* me life… I dunno where I'd be without ya."

"I know where *I'd* be."

"Where's that?"

"Waitin' for *ye*."

She snuggled in, their lips pressed, and Winslow's mind flashed to the first time he saw her in that seaside pub, the stories they traded, and the kiss they shared on that moonlit beach, as all his memories converged on the present moment.

She drifted back and contended, "We saved each other, by the way. N' I think *I* was the lucky one." When her husband's eyebrows arched, she brushed his blond curls and petted his bearded cheek. "With your charms, ye'd steal another girl's heart, I'm sure."

Winslow watched her. The setting sun was no competition to her ruby locks; the rolling, Scottish waters were no competition to her maritime eyes; and the harmonious tones of larksong on the springtime breeze held no candle to her lilted, angelic whispers. Anna Meria Lough was the finest woman he'd ever known.

"Naw," he avowed, clearing mist from his eyes. "I think I did alright the first time around." He pushed off his seat to stand, feeling stiffer than his younger body was used to, but Anna floated in his guiding hand to join him in embrace. "Are ya ready, dear?"

She hugged him warmly and answered.

Tears flowed free from the old fisherman's eyes as he pulled back, and viewed the smooth, blue urn he cradled in his arms. He traced the single word etched on its surface, and heard her pretty voice pierce time, like heavenly chimes on the wind, to match its engraving:

Always.

Winslow patted the urn, shaking a little. He fought tears and steadied himself with a soothing breath, retrieving a memory, and finding a promise. He nodded with resolution, then opened the lid, and freed the ashes.

Winslow watched them twinkle like stardust and spiral as one with the blue, then sat back with the empty container. Below the epitaph, an additional decoration was carved: a small icon in the likeness of a seal.

"Happy anniversary, Anna," he said.

A breeze petted his back, as the water's surface stilled. In the moment of silence that followed, he inspected the currents, then the clouds. He waited a moment, nodded again, then looped some rope, and pulled the oars.

Oddly, however, the boat didn't budge. Winslow's brow stitched. He tried again. Still, nothing. He looked over his shoulder at a swaying branch on the bank, then saw a shimmer of mist condense above the water. His eyes glinted.

The locked rowboat rose a foot, then splashed down again before a surge of bubbles rumbled and a smash of loch water hit, washing Winslow flat in the center of the rocking craft. The long neck of a legendary visitor stretched high beyond him, and her smooth head cocked with a curious hum.

Winslow's chest puffed, awestruck, before he cracked a gallant grin. "Can't say I'm surprised."

The Everlovin'
Loch Ness Monster

er off yer rocker, Wins—there's no way!" the red-faced cook erupted.

The fisherman shrugged, as passersby lit up outside, hands waved, and an audience of excited Bayfielders flowed into the restaurant, eager to hear what wonders Winslow Hoffner had smuggled back with him from his trip.

"Alright, fine," he conceded. "I was a *smidge* surprised."

"That *ain't* what I'm talkin' about!"

Patrons squeezed in. Muirin scooted through as the elated listeners, whose faces were plastered with glittery, childlike giddiness, each flagged her down like moviegoers requesting snacks for a show.

"You're tryin' to tell me that the *one day* ye go on holiday the everlovin' *Loch Ness Monster* shows up?!"

The audience gasped and murmured.

"I ain't *tryin'*, I'm *tellin'*," Winslow chuckled. "Sounds t'me like yer havin' a hard time *believin'*."

"Oh, ye don't say!" Ken squeaked.

"What did it look like, Winslow?" Linda Cunningham asked, dazzled, before her children jumped in rowdily with their own inquiries:

Luke hopped. "How big was it?"

" 'Bout as tall as this here restaurant."

"*Whoa!*"

"Did it have sharp teeth?" Lily added.

"Darn tootin'!" Winslow curled his fingers by his mouth and mimicked the monster's booming call.

The kids laughed.

Ken crossed his arms. "Ye sure it wasn't a *log*?"

Muirin poked him.

"*Ach!*"

"A snarlin' log would be a sight all its own," Winslow chuckled. "But I ain't been surer 'bout anythin', Keel."

Reba Belle-Isle pulled in a chair. "*Amazing* things just keep happening around you, huh?"

Winslow shrugged. "I reckon amazin' things happen every day, Belle…"

John Chaplain and Becci Hamrin sat in the puttering, damaged truck, as border agents looked over their odd cargo.

"What's that, eh?" one asked.

"Art," Becci tried the lie again, as the men looked over the Thingamajig in the bed.

"And what's *this?*" asked the other.

The Canvey Island Monster was possuming in the backseat, stiff as a board with her mouth gaped, like some monstrous, freaky sculpture.

Becci swallowed. "Also art."

When the agent turned away, the little creature twitched. Becci shot a freezing look at her, as the man circled around, and through the open window, his gloved hand reached.

"You can't bring this over the border."

John's throat tightened, as did his grip on the wheel. *We're screwed*, he thought. But to his utter shock, the guard's fingers reached into the vent grate on the air conditioner and snagged the buttercup flower Becci had picked.

"No foreign plants."

"Really?" John felt himself say.

"We're sorry," Becci said quickly.

John gawped at the friendly guard, who nodded and said, "It's an obscure rule," holding the flower under his chin. "Have a good day."

Winslow completed his thought, "Long as yer payin' attention, that is."

" *'Ey, Wins is back!"* another rejoice came from the incoming crowd, as Barnaby Smithins and even more patrons flowed in and packed around the fisherman's seat at the bar.

Winslow smiled gently at the warm reception of his friends as they grouped up to hear his tale.

Ken gave a quick smile too, one made from a blend of familiarity and incredulity, before he shook his head and challenged, "You're outta your mind, friend."

"Maybe I am." Winslow inspected the walls, looking lost. "Ya changed the whole restaurant again — I hardly recognize the place!"

"Oh, here it comes."

Winslow smiled. "I like it."

"Huh. That *is* a shock." Ken paced to grab more menus, giving the bargoers time to scooch in chairs.

Meanwhile, Winslow's gaze swept over Ken's nautical décor, finding that in the days he'd been gone the display had been vastly updated, strikingly less chaotic than before and featuring new photographs of families, placid portraits of Bayfield's landmarks done by local artists, and amid it all, strings of warm, purple lights that bathed the cozy space in dawn-colored splendor. Winslow couldn't find the old rowboat painting, but instead came upon a classic photo of himself and Hank hauling in netfuls of fish for Ken's father, next to another picture of the sailors posing beside Ken and Muirin at the ribbon-cutting ceremony of the eatery's grand reopening.

Winslow lifted his chin to the photographs. "I think those're me new favorites."

Ken nodded. "Mine too."

Peeling from the counter, Sal "Sleepy" Hurly emerged before the crowd, smacking his dry lips and glancing bewilderedly at the sudden activity around him. "I di'n't miss a new story, did I?"

"Naw, Sleepy, yer just in time," Winslow said.

"Oh, good." He waggled a hand at Ken. "A drink!"

"I think ye've had enough, friend."

"Not for me." He clapped Winslow's shoulder. "For the storyteller!"

A tall, glass mug clunked down, dark, fizzing liquid sloshing with a sizable cap of foam on the surface, just enough for a cluster of creamy bubbles to sway and cascade over the edge. Winslow lapped it up, sipped, and energized, clearing his gray whiskers with a swipe of his sleeve, as his icy eye struck his growing audience.

"So, here's what happened…"

Winslow caught the newcomers up on his encounter thus far, standing and waving his hands like a painter as he detailed the explosive arrival of the legendary beast; his little rowboat catching on the hump of her back and crashing down in a rocky sway; the monster's long neck tangling in the boat's mooring rope to swerve high above and sing; and the cool pitter-patter of loch water raining from the giant's whiskery chin. Winslow touched the phantom sensation of droplets on his cheek, before expounding:

"Best believe, this critter's reputation preceded her, but she was makin' quite the audition nonetheless."

"Audition for what?" Ken asked.

"Ta make it inta me journal!" Winslow lifted the worn, leather-bound tome from his travel bag, with its wrinkled, ancient-looking parchment pages and old, wooden plaque affixed to its cover: the Journal of Curiosities. "She was hittin' all the classic moves, o'course. Took me on a lightnin'-fast tour 'cross her loch, had me coastin' n' splashin' left n' right, up n' down." Winslow sipped and smacked. "Nessie moved so quick she made her own waves fer me ta surf, n' I was hangin' *twenty* just tryin' ta hang on!"

Muirin recognized the journal on the counter and made a rickety gasp. Her fingers touched on the faded cover and curling, water-damaged pages. "Winslow, what happened t'yer book?"

With a high eyebrow, Ken added, "Looks like ye fished the thing out yerself."

Winslow nodded. "Aye, it got dunked. I had it with me when Nessie decided ta dive."

The room made a collective sound of shock.

"Yep. This was the *second* half o' her audition! In the scramble, the ropes got tangled up in the thwarts n' oarlocks, so when Nessie decided ta take a nosedive the boat was strung up behind her like a wooden parachute, n' I was right there, clingin' in the air pocket in-between!"

"That must've been terrifying!" Reba gasped.

"Certainly gave me a start at first." Winslow sipped.

"What did you see down there?" Barnaby piped.

"I'd say I caught a glimpse o' the world from her perspective fer a spell. The water was bluer'n I ever recalled, the white bubbles was twirlin' by like li'l dancers. *Everythin'* in her realm was glitterin'… It was beautiful." Winslow blinked free. "Though, t'be fair, it coulda been all the blood rushin' ta me head, too."

His audience giggled.

"I was *sure* I was 'bout ta pass out, in fact, when I saw me surroundin's pulse, twirl, n' warp. Looked like a tunnel was closin' in."

"I know the feelin'," Sleepy said woozily.

"Turned out it *was* a tunnel!"

"Oh, lucky!"

"Aye," Winslow snorted.

"A tunnel to *where?*" Ken interjected.

"Ta her cave!" Winslow sparkled. "Part *three* o' her audition! We spiraled through this narrow tube o' rocks ta find this pretty, underwater alcove."

"How'd the boat make it through?"

"It didn't. It exploded."

"Ah. Gotcha."

Listeners jumped in their seats as Winslow threw open his arms and reenacted the blast. "*POW!* Smithereens! This li'l rental weren't made ta be dragged by a loch monster, if ya can believe."

Ken smiled. "That *is* hard to believe."

"Right? All the splinters got stuck in me jacket. Had ta buy me a new one from the gift shop later." He tugged on the hem of his fresh, sporty, blue-and-white windbreaker. The Scottish flag was embroidered on the left chest pocket.

"Looking suave!" Reba said.

"Aye, I thought so." Winslow swaggered. "Somethin' new." He bopped, posing. "I liked it."

"Have to admit," Ken shook his head, "the fact that ye changed up yer style for *any* reason is the most compellin' part o' yer story so far."

"Did you bring back anything else?" Lily asked, she and her brother perking up at the mention of the gift shop.

"*Hm*," Winslow thought. "I prolly should've, but I gots a bit distracted pickin' all *these* outta me pockets…" Winslow produced two handfuls of wooden scraps and clattered them onto the counter. Everyone dove in to inspect them.

Ken pointed. "Are those — ?"

"Bits o' the boat? Yep."

The listeners snatched up the artifacts, literal puzzle pieces to Winslow's mysterious account. "These is the least sharp o' the pieces, but be careful anyhow. I figured the dockmaster wouldn't miss 'em. Ya can help yerselves; I gots plenty."

Ken held a piece up. He waved it. "More props. *Very* elaborate," he complimented.

Winslow made a gappy grin.

"What happened next?!" Sleepy hurrahed.

"Well, I clambered outta the waterhole, caught me breath, n' took a look around. It was a fancy spot the beastie had picked. Full o' these shimmery, blue crystals. Real posh."

"Crystals."   Ken waggled the boat fragment. "Aye, let's see us one o' *those*, eh?"

"Sure!"

"Oh brother, I shouldn't have asked…"

Winslow unzipped his chest pocket and produced the sample on cue. He handed it to his friend and the crowd *oohed* as they beheld the twinkling, quartzy, sapphire gem Ken turned in his left hand. That, alongside the boat piece in his right won over nearly everyone in the restaurant.

"Hoardin' treasure!" Sleepy hurrahed.   "Just like that giant lobster did, eh, Wins?"

"S'pose so," the fisherman agreed.

"*Mighty* similar," the cook muttered, before others leaned in with more vociferous approval.

"Well I'll be," Reba grinned.

"Gorgeous," Muirin gushed.

"I'm sold!" Barnaby slapped the counter.

Ken turned red, blown away by the acceptance, as Winslow nudged him impishly.

"Pretty cool, eh?"

Ken steamed, "This is just a bunch o' sticks n' stones!"

"Aye, but yer words can never hurt me."

"*Ha!*" Sleepy busted a gut.

The crimson faded from Ken's cheeks. He groaned, half-laughing, "Ye *are* extra prepared."

"Yer extra skeptical."

"Eh, it's been a few days. I was goin' through withdrawals."

"Same," Winslow chuckled. To complete the trifecta, he opened his fabled journal. He took a sugary swig to soak his throat, then continued. "So, after I gots the ropes offa the beastie, she sung a little. Real sweet tune, 'specially the way it echoed. I was feelin' inspired, so I hung out fer a bit... *heh,* not that I had much of a choice," Winslow admitted. "But, if I *could* choose, I wouldn't choose ta be anywhere else. What light came through was playin' offa the gems real quaintly, so I gots out me journal n' got ta sketchin'."

Muirin looked over Winslow's shoulder, relieved. "The center o' the pages stayed dry?"

"Aye, fer the most part. It was sealed tight in this new satchel I bought, so that took most o' the water, but not all o' it. 'Parently 'waterproof' ain't 'monster-proof.' " Winslow laughed, smoothing the wiggly parchment down on the latest entry and showing them an inky rendition of a swan-necked loch monster in a crystalline cave.

Amid the murmurs of approval, Sleepy's voice rose, "Clearest picture o' the beast *I've* ever seen."

"It's a *drawin'*, Sleepy," Ken said.

Muirin poked her son, less sharply than usual, and he smiled and amended:

"A darn good one to be true."

"Thanks, Keel."

Muirin patted the fisherman's shoulder. "Ye've had that book *forever*. Glad it wasn't ruined."

"Yeah, came out alright all things considered, didn't it? 'Sides, I like it better this way! It's been through *legendary* waters." Winslow patted it and smiled. "There's magic in them pages."

The room broke into whimsical side conversations. Some beer was dribbled by zealous listeners. Ken wiped the counter as Sleepy grabbed his arm, asking, "Pretty remarkable, hm?"

Winslow straightened up with a proud smile.

"Well," Ken sighed, "I suppose after *everythin'* ye've told us, gettin' all chummy with a modern-day plesiosaur ain't *too* far-fetched."

Winslow finished his drink and smacked. "Weren't a plesiosaur."

"Beg yer pardon?"

"Weren't a plesiosaur," he repeated.

"But ye *said* it was a plesiosaur."

"I never said that."

He prodded the picture. "Then what's *that?!*"

"That's Nessie."

"What!" Ken raged. He pinched the space between his eyes. He breathed, then composed. "Now, even *I* know this myth, Wins. It's famous! Big dinosaur cooped up in the loch."

"Aye, I thought the same. Even at first glance the critter looked like ya'd expect—smooth, snaky." He lifted his lips. "Big ol' fangs! *RAH!*"

The younger listeners glittered with excitement.

"She was even green!" Winslow continued. "But she weren't no dino."

Ken looked baffled. "Then what *was* she?"

Winslow smiled. "She was a seal."

John adjusted his glasses as he stepped into Milly Matterhorn's Museum of Maritime Marvels, greeted by a rack of custom cryptid postcards. One featured a silvery, seal-like creature with three eyes and tusks, barking beneath bold, swirly lettering that read, *See the Sights at Muskrat Lake!*

That's a new one, John thought.

A door clattered open and the museum's titular countess appeared. "Greetings landwalk—*Oh!* John, Becci, you made it! You're *alive!*" Her silver fillings flashed as she beamed a huge grin and clapped, then called for her husband, "*Peter!* I told you they'd make it!"

"We brought something..." Becci stepped in, cradling a swaddled Canvey Island Monster. "We're in over our heads a little." When she unwrapped the tiny beast, she was possuming again, perfectly rigid.

"A new display!" Milly elated. "Oh, it's so realistic." She reached out to take it.

"It *is* real," Becci said.

Milly's eyes widened. "A *real* cryptid taxidermy..."

"No, she's—"

The beast gurgled and sprang alive.

"*AH!*" Milly screamed. "What in the—?!"

The Canvey Island Monster bounded around the museum as Milly held her chest.

"Where'd she come from?"

"Hangar 19," John revealed, holding Milly's arm. "Sorry, Milly, we—"

"Sorry? What're you sorry for? I love her!"

John's eyes flicked at Becci. "Yeah, she has that effect on people, I noticed."

Milly knelt to follow the walking fish's antics. "What's her name?"

"She doesn't have a—"

"Buttercup," Becci answered.

"Uh, Buttercup," John said. "Apparently."

Becci grinned, as the creature bounced into the backroom, where Peter could be heard, screaming, "*AH! Sweet Lord! What is that?!*"

"Buttercup," Milly answered calmly. "She's a Canvey Island Monster."

John lit up at her immediate knowledge of the animal. "You've heard of them?"

"Oh, sure! Winslow taught me all about these little critters. He has a *great* entry on 'em. Ask to read it in his journal sometime."

"Will do."

Milly petted the scaly, clicking creature when it returned to her. "Does she need a place to stay?"

Becci exchanged stunned looks with John, then asked, "Would you *really* be willing to take her in?"

"Are you *kidding*? She's a living jumpscare! She'd be perfect for the back room!"

"Don't tell me we're becoming a *zoo* now!" Peter wailed.

John and Becci laughed.

"I promise ya, this beastie was a *seal!*" Winslow got close, as Ken's face stretched, boggled by his friend's insistence and intensity. "N' I *know* seals!" The fisherman's buggy eye quivered. The brief staring contest was followed by the quick, quiet lines:

"What'cha mean?"

"Don't worry about it."

Lily raised her hand and asked, "Um, how'd you get *out* of the cave?"

"Good question," Ken said.

"*Great* question!" Winslow clapped. "Nessie was draggin' back inta the waterhole, y'see. I reckoned we gained some trust, so I went ta climb on her back. But, turns out this beastie took an even greater shine t'me than I realized, 'cause she went n' scooped me up with her snout, then went rocketin' back through the tunnel!

"I busted through the surface o' the loch, the air, n' finally a layer o' sparklin' mist, afore me eyes struck the Scottish sky. Someone up there musta gotten their times mixed up, 'cause I swear, the clouds was painted like dawn again. Violet, ruby, n' gold. Just perfect. N' the feelin' I felt there was more precious than any o' them crystals, I promise ya. Ain't felt that type o' calm since..." His eyes flowed to the spot where the rowboat painting once hung, but found the new photos again instead. He grinned. "Well, I guess the takeaway is it's *always* been with me, somewhere."

Uproarious applause filled the restaurant. The kids cheered and their mother thanked the fisherman for another incredible tale. Reba clapped and whistled. Barnaby pointed and proclaimed this to be his favorite thus far.

Amid the cheers, Ken leaned in to ask, "How could *no one else* see this?"

"I dunno." Winslow shrugged. "Maybe they did!"

"That'd be *global* news, Wins."

Sleepy stretched across the counter for the remote. "Check the telly!"

Ken rolled his eyes and pushed him the control. "Knock yerself out."

Winslow found one more sip in his mug and polished it off. "*Mm.* That's good." He clomped the empty container down. "Thanks fer treatin', Sleepy."

"Hm? Oh, anytime, Wins," Sleepy said, briefly breaking his trance before returning to the television to blearily switch between channels. "Ya deserve it."

And as Ken dragged in the empty mug, Winslow nodded, "Thanks fer stockin' up on the good stuff, Keel."

"Yer the only reason I keep it on tap, friend."

Winslow stood to make his exit. "My ride oughtta be here soon," he said.

"I'll meet ye outside in a second," Ken called. "Don't go nowhere yet."

"Alright." Winslow strolled with his hands in his pockets and nodded to friends, who patted his shoulders and thanked him for the story. He thanked them for listening in kind, then pushed through the exit, smelled the cool, salty air, smiled, and stepped out.

Ken sifted under the counter, searching for something. *"Ah, here it is…"*

"KEN!" Sleepy hollered.

The cook shot up, banging his head on the underside of the counter. *"Argh!* Sleepy, what is it?!"

"Look! *Look!"*

Ken looked. His face dropped.

A story on an obscure international news channel showed a blurry picture of a monstrous form. The restaurant broke into excited mutterings as Ken pushed up to the front to squint. The lower third boasted the image as, *New Evidence of Loch Ness' Oldest Legend*, as the newscaster pointed out that some remained unconvinced, due to the strange shape protruding from the creature's head.

Everyone leaned in. The shape she referred to looked just like a man sitting on the beast's snout.

Sleepy pointed. "Don't that look like Winslow?"

"No way." Ken's face twitched. He grabbed the screen and checked behind it. "No way..." His cheeks flushed red and his eyes grew wild. "Are ye *in* on this?!"

Sleepy's beard flapped as he opened his arms and shook his head, while the cook gripped the TV and searched it high and low again. The rest of the room thundered with exultation and amazement.

"There he is!" Reba screamed.

"Record!" Sleepy hollered, scouring for the button. "*Record!*"

"This is the single greatest day in the history o' this town!" Barnaby boomed.

"Ain't no doubtin' it!" Muirin agreed. "That's our Winslow Hoffner!"

Ken wailed, "Oh, ye've *gotta* be kidding me!"

The Storyteller

ohn Chaplain and Becci Hamrin swerved down the winding, beachside road in the vintage, red pickup as the bay waved to welcome them home. Glinting, gold reflections of the setting sun flashed on the water's glassy peaks, as the dusking sky blushed with warm violet and embery crimson. John rolled down the windows to feel the familiar chill and smell the salty brine on the air.

We made it, he thought. He rested an elbow on the open window, coppery-brown hair buffeting freely in the pelagic breezes. At the sound of a pen scratching, he checked the passenger seat and saw Becci scrawling a closing sentence in a notepad, then stamping a proud period at the end.

"There!" she said. "Perfect."

"You finished the story already?"

"Yep. Took some of *your* stuff, some of *my* stuff." She laced her fingers. "Worked my magic, and *boom*. Another one for the column!"

"Albert will be thrilled."

Becci chuckled, "Nell won't."

"Oh, right." John's face stretched, as the debacles from the previous week returned in his mind. He hadn't thought about the drama at the Messenger in a long time. But, the tense memory was eclipsed by a prevailing buzz of excitement, and adventure. He shrugged. "*Ah.* What does he know?"

Becci's cheeks dimpled at his tenor. "Maybe he can write a poem about it."

Just then, John's phone rang. It was their assistant editor.

Becci's eyes got wide. "I shouldn't have said his name, should I?" Her partner took a breath as his thumb hovered over the button. Becci smoothed her hair and coat, mumbling, "*What, does he have this place* bugged *or something?*"

John answered the call and put it on speaker, "Hey, Nell. We're just getting ba—"

"Johnny. Hi. Great. Listen, I got the pictures Mrs. McCottry sent in."

"…Mrs. McCottry sent pictures?"

"Yeah. Of the *'man in black,'* " Nell grumbled. "Seriously, who do you think is going to buy this?"

"*The cake worked,*" Becci whispered.

"And what's with the barrage of phone calls I've been getting about a *'Metal Man?'* "

John glanced right, confused. Becci shrugged. He answered, "I'm sorry, Nell, I don't know. This is the first I'm hearing about it."

Nell steamed, "I want you and Beck to stop playing coy and come in early tomorrow to sort through all this! I…" The sound of annoyed paper-shuffling preceded a growl. "My desk looks like it's covered in pulp magazine covers—!"

John did his best to defuse the situation, but the assistant editor talked in circles, before completely blowing a gasket and hanging up in a huff. John looked at Becci, astonished. "We leave town and everything just gets *weirder.*"

Becci pointed. "But the leads are coming from *other* people, now!"

John rubbed his chin. "Huh."

Becci cheered, "Job security!"

John caught her high-five and laughed. "Maybe… Nell seemed pretty pissed, though."

"What else is new?"

John eased, thinking. "But yeah, we do have a bunch of leads coming in now, don't we?"

"Uh, *yeah*." Becci found her pen behind her ear and flipped open her pad, cross-referencing notes with the papers she discovered in Hangar 19. She scribbled, narrating, "Okay… first story's done. That's the agent sightings and the deep dive on the Cryptolabe." She circled something and scratched an arrow into the margin with another idea. "Why don't we follow up on that metal guy next; that sounds pretty sweet…"

John smiled warmly as he watched her passion spill onto the page.

She brushed a strawberry tress behind her ear. "Okay, and then… that—" She pointed with her pen to the Thingamajig joggling in the truck's bed. "*That's* going in part three!"

"Yeah?"

"*Oh*, yeah. Whatever Winslow's planning to use it for, you *know* that's gonna be newsworthy." She clicked her pen. "I've got a feeling."

John checked the enthusiasm in her olivine eyes. "That's good enough for me," he said. "You were right about everything else."

Becci sat back. "Hey, I was, wasn't I?" She flipped her notepad shut and rested her hands behind her head, enjoying the reflective peaks of the bay dancing with the setting sun's warm, triumphant hues. "Told ya everything would work out in the end."

As Winslow Hoffner stepped outside, the riotous applause from the eatery only seemed to escalate.

He staggered at the noise. "*Wow, they really liked that'n,*" he muttered, thrilled.

It took a while for Ken Keeley to work his way through the bombastic mob and make it outside. He panted, the red hair on his head floofed out.

Winslow nodded to him. "Y'alright?"

"Yeah, yeah."

"Y'sure?"

"*Yeah.*" Ken sucked a breath through his nose and touched his throbbing neck. "Yeah, I'm good,

Wins. That—" He gestured behind him with his thumb. "*That* was good." He chuckled a little.

"Ah, thanks, Keel. Glad ya enjoyed."

Ken rambled on breathlessly as he smoothed his hair, which kept popping back up. "It really was. That was really a good'n, ye oughtta be proud."

" 'Preciate it."

"I won't ask *how* ye managed to pull off that last bit at the moment…" Ken said.

Winslow looked confused.

The cook continued, "Right now, I just wanna give ye this before I forget." He handed his friend a small, square present. The wrapping was decorated with cartoon balloons, hats, and cakes.

"It ain't me birthday, Keeley."

"That's the only wrapping I had, just open it."

Winslow unwrapped it, and when the gift surfaced, his eye twitched and shined. It was the rowboat painting.

As Ken watched a smile etch his friend's face, the rambunctious sounds from the eatery behind him seemed to fade. Accompanying the gift was a small, handwritten note that read:

For the memories ye cherish

that inspire us all to dream,

for the friendship ye gave me family

when I was but a teen,

for all o' your high-sailing adventures

that delight us every week,

for ye and Anna,

Happy Anniversary.

Your pal,

Ken

Winslow hugged him. Ken puffed startledly as he was squeezed, then laughed and patted the man's back.

"Yer a good friend, Keeley."

"You too, Wins."

"Gonna needs a frame."

"It's got a frame."

"Not fer the paintin'. Fer the card!"

Ken's chest swelled with pride. "Aye, I was proud o' that rhyme. Not too shabby, eh?"

"Aye. *Plus...*" Winslow pointed to the third-to-last line. "Handwritten *proof* ya like me stories! *Ha!*"

"Oh, brother—"

"That's goin' on me wall fer sure."

"*What've I done...*" Ken joked under his breath. After a while, the cook tapped his foot, glanced back at the eatery, then caved and asked, "Alright. It's killin' me. How'd ye do the last bit on the TV?"

"Hm?"

"The TV! Not to shatter the illusion or anythin', but that was some next-level stuff, Wins. Not to mention gettin' Sleepy of all people onboard—*hoh!* Now *there's* a triumph o' actin'!" He laughed.

Winslow angled an eye at him. "Come again?"

Ken raised an eyebrow back. "The news clip."

Winslow blinked, baffled. "Whaddaya mean?"

Ken raved, "Whaddaye mean, '*whaddaya mean?*' The newscaster! The picture on the screen—!"

The exchange halted when John and Becci rolled up in Winslow's squeaking red truck, lugging the weighty Thingamajig. The journalists beamed big, cheery grins from the front seats, equal parts bleary and accomplished, and waved.

Winslow smiled. "They did it!" As the pickup squealed and puttered to a rickety stop, the fisherman and the cook were shadowed by the half-tarped, bewildering contraption. "Hm. It's bigger'n I remembered…"

John and Becci stepped out, stretched, and exchanged joyous hugs and salutations with the fisherman, while Ken's features glued to the odd object they'd brought back with them, its peg-coils sprouting from the holey cloth. "Wins…"

"Yeah?"

"What's that?"

"Would ya believe me if I told ya it was a force field generator?"

"No."

"Well, that's about as much belief as I can pull outta ya normally, so," Winslow snorted, "let's just go with that."

The cook frowned, baffled, and before he could craft another sentence, a second vehicle rumbled in, towing an even more-enormous, tarped cargo.

Hank Malloy rolled down his window and greeted them with gusto, "Ahoy, folks!"

With all the developments outdoors, the heads of those inside the restaurant began to turn, and steadily Bayfielders crept from Keeley's Bayside Eatery to investigate what new mysteries were percolating out there.   John and Becci joined Winslow and Ken in fascination of Hank's surprise.

"Whatcha got there, Hank?" Winslow asked.

"I did it," Hank glimmered giddily. "I *finally* did it!"

A look of realization flashed in Winslow's eyes and he laughed, joining in the celebration already, while John and Becci shrugged, and the curiosity of the onlookers deepened.

Ken called, "*What?* What did ye do?"

Hank smiled and pulled a loop to unveil it, revealing a watertight hatch; metal panels, painted yellow; and a sleek, dome-shaped glass face, through which seating and top-of-the-line controls were visible.

Ken's face stretched in shock again. "Ye... ye bought a — ?"

"Aye, tha's right!" Hank cut in, too excited. "I bought a *submarine*!"

Gasps and murmurs sounded, while Ken pressed, "How could ye *ever* afford it?"

"Oh, it's a funny story," Hank said. "While back, Wins n' I found this cave full o' gold..."

Ken's eyebrows arched. He remembered.

"I don' wanna spoil how we got there since Wins tells it the best, but I *will* say it involves a giant—"

"*Lobster?*"

"Aye, so ye have heard it!"

Ken wobbled, as the townsfolk flowed around him to observe the wonders. He caught his balance. "*I'm… going to bed.*"

Becci tucked her hands in her coat pockets and rocked, glimpsing the sleek, personal submarine. "You kinda stole our thunder there, huh, Hank?"

Hank laughed, "*Heh.* Sorry about tha'."

But among a few onlookers, including the fishermen, inquisitive looks soon glided back to Winslow's pickup, primarily at a set of three clawmarks raked through the steel of the driver's side door.

"*Oh, yeah…*" Becci remembered.

She and John cringed as Winslow ambled over, bent his knees, and surveyed the damages. His gray eyebrows arched.

"What happened ta Ol' Red, eh?"

John gulped and he apologized, then explained, "It's a long story."

Winslow touched the marks.

The journalists braced. But they quickly eased, when, instead of any kind of ire, he returned a look of good humor, and elation. The fisherman's eye glittered proudly above his gappy smile, as he leaned in to reply:

"I'm all ears."

About the Author

Michael Thompson is an award-winning author and illustrator from Northern Virginia. His novels, *World of the Orb* and *Winslow Hoffner's Incredible Encounters*, each earned international acclaim in the *Feathered Quill Book Awards*.

With his latest publication, Michael carries on a tradition of fast-paced storytelling, witty dialogue, and memorable characters; marks the first exciting sequel to his folkloric fantasy series; and looks ahead to sharing the next mythical adventures of the gallant fisherman, Winslow Hoffner.

For more information and a complete list of Michael's award-winning works, visit:

MichaelThompsonBooks.com

www.ingramcontent.com/pod-product-compliance
Lightning Source LLC
Chambersburg PA
CBHW060752190726
48285CB00002B/397